D0510932

ACKNOWLEDGEMENTS

The day I emailed my manuscript to Hashtag Press, the universe must've finally heard my whispers because into my life came Abiola Bello and Helen Lewis, two women who are passionate about everything that they do and lovely with it. They got my writing. They got my vision for I am Winter. And they set about making my dream of becoming a published author a reality. I would never have done it without you. Thank you!

To Anne Glenn for this beautiful cover. Thank you!

Growing up, I was an avid reader of anything I could get my hands on. I adored Dr Seuss and Henry Wadsworth Longfellow, and I'm pretty sure my dad was called into school one time to explain to my primary school teacher why he allowed seven-year-old me to read what she called 'saucy limericks' in the newspaper, which I had faithfully recreated in my exercise book. Without this love of books and reading, I might never have written my own. Thank you!

Over the years, my children have learnt to understand that my vacant expression during conversations means that I'm watching a character in my head doing something unexpected that I need to write down. They've been patient. They've been supportive. They've believed in me the way that I believe in them, even when I forgot to buy new school shoes. To Dan, Jade, Ruby, Maxime, and Meghann, the biggest thank you of all! You are my world.

Lastly, to Anne Glennie and Helen MacKinven for the gift of this book's title, it's perfect. Thank you!

For my children

PROLOGUE

Cee was nine months older than me. We were in the same year at primary school—there were only twenty-three of us so our hands couldn't help touching when we did the hokey-cokey—but we weren't friends.

She was loud and embarrassing and bossy. If there was any performing to be done, Cee was at the front of the class with a hand up in the air, the words to 'It's a Hard-Knock Life' already tumbling out of her mouth. At Christmas nativity in the village church, she played Mary or an angel or both. It didn't matter to her so long as she was seen and heard. Sports Day she took part in everything. When parents were invited in to 'Show and Tell' or Mother's Day tea parties, Cee invented an invisible family to make up for the lack of real family in attendance and gave them weird names like Archibald and Elizabetta and Geraldine, poured them tea in plastic cups, and kept up a steady stream of conversation about visiting her grandmother in London, where Great-Uncle Jimmy slipped and broke his neck one winter when the weather was Baltic.

She lived in a fantasy world and no one else was allowed in. Apart from her big brother Ritchie. Cee and Ritchie were like shoes and socks or Jedward, weird when they weren't together or close to each other. I'd have been her friend sooner if it would've made Ritchie see past my ankle socks and pleated skirts and look at me the way he and his mates looked at my mum. I loved Ritchie more than I loved Harry Styles. He had brown skin and curly hair and there was something about the way he walked around with his hood always up that made me feel like the ground was trembling under my feet.

The summer I turned eleven, it seemed Cee lived outside on the walkway linking our houses, with Ritchie circling on his bike or huddled on the grass with his mates pretending they weren't sharing a smoke or pictures of tits.

"That girl's always outside," Gran said whenever her leather trousers squeaked through the front door. "Her mother's obviously got no time for her."

I asked if could go out to play. My best friend was on holiday on an island, the name of which I'd forgotten as soon as she told me, and although she promised to bring me back a seashell or a dolphin to put in my ballerina box, her absence left my chest wide open and infected with a sense of abandonment.

"Course you can, sweetheart," Gran said. "It'll do you good to get out."

Mum checked the mileage on her exercise bike odometer. Sweat dripped from the end of her nose and she brushed it with the back of her hand. Her legs kept moving.

I sat on the step outside our house and smiled at Cee. She came straight over.

"Do you want to go to the park?" she asked.

I shrugged. It was the first time I'd been anywhere without telling my mum, which meant that "Any Tom, Dick, or Harry could pounce on you and no one would know where to look"; that's something Gran would say.

We walked. Cee talked. She told me Ritchie was going to move away, live with his dad in a shiny apartment in Glasgow. When he was settled, he'd come back and get her and she'd get a proper education, go to college, and become a policewoman.

"You can see me with a gun, can't you?" she asked.

I didn't know what to say because I thought her arms were too skinny to hold a gun, and her hair was so long it might get caught in the trigger and rip bald patches in her scalp, and then she'd look like she had alopecia which was Gran's nightmare because her sister had it. So, I didn't say anything.

My silence made her roll her eyes.

"Well, I'm not staying here."

"What about your mum?"

"She'll only miss me when the baby cries."

We passed the woods. We kept right on going until we reached the park at the bottom of the hill, sat on the very top of the climbing frame, our legs dangling and my heart rushing too fast with the fear of falling and breaking my neck and ending up with a wonky head. Cee told me she'd seen her mum having sex with a man.

"They were on the living room floor. She still had her shoes on, and her knees jiggled when his bum slapped on top of her and after, she had carpet burns on her back. She showed Sam and Sam called them battle scars."

"Who's Sam?" I asked. I didn't really care who Sam was, I was just buying time, incubating the shared secret until it became a tangible thing, a rope binding us together. It didn't occur to me she might have told this story to anyone else. This was our special moment, the spark that would ignite our friendship and from then on, we would be inseparable.

Or so I thought.

"Sam's her mate. She's a lesbian."

To me, wobbling in the breeze, my knuckles white around the climbing frame, Cee was a warrior princess, fearless, strong, honest. My brain was humming with panic, sifting through the fragments of my life trying to choose one secret that might live up to Cee's, one special moment that would seal the deal, unite us forever.

And of all the things I could've possibly mentioned, I told her about my bear-wolf. I blurted it out, confident in my newfound friendship and my closeness to the clouds. I told her about all the trinkets the creature kept safe for me, about the ball stuffed with beads from my mum's necklace, and *The Hunger Games* book my friend gave me, and how one day I'd live in the woods and eat nuts and wild mushrooms—although I didn't like mushrooms yet, but I would do when I was older. I'd never trusted anyone enough to tell before now. But there on the climbing frame, the backs of our legs metal-chilled, I believed Cee was the same as me. I believed I'd discovered a kindred spirit.

"You actually think you found a bear-wolf?" she asked. "What even is that?" Her eyebrows arched and I felt silly because I could've told her I'd seen my mum having sex too.

"It lives in the woods. I thought it was a dog, but she's furry like a bear."

Cee blinked slowly and I felt like I was losing her, my euphoria being replaced by twisting cramps in my stomach.

"She's real," I said.

Thunderclouds rolled in, purple grey, booming like elephants.

"My brother Ritchie loves storms," she said jumping down onto bark chips, her hair flying behind her.

I climbed down the steps with the rusty paint, holding onto the rails like a child.

4

"Run!" she yelled, giggling as fat drops of rain dotted our clothes and our hair. We were drenched before we reached the main road; I could see her bra through her white T-shirt, and I wished I'd worn one of the white lacy bras Mum had bought me from Primark.

It was still chucking it down when I stopped at the door to our house and waited for Cee to say goodbye, but she kept on running till she reached her own front door where she fumbled for a key in her pocket and let herself in without glancing behind her.

That summer I didn't go back to the park with Cee. The next day, on the walkway outside our houses, someone had drawn chalk pictures of a flat-haired stick-girl holding hands with a long-tailed bear.

1

I can hear Mum's voice as I tiptoe up the stairs from my bedroom which is on the lower floor of our house. On the top step, I stop, my back pressed against the wall so that if she is walking about in the living room, she won't see me.

"When's Dad going to look at the new fish tank?" She's talking to Gran. They're not interested in Grandad's fish; my mum will be calculating how much money he's spending, and Gran will be working out when she can have some alone time with the telly remote.

Gran's voice is quiet which means she's sitting at the table at the far end of the room, and I can't smell cigarettes which means that Mum isn't standing at the back door pretending that holding the fag outside means no smoke enters the house.

I bound the two steps between the stairs and the kitchen and find Mum's purse on the side where the bills and bank statements and hair salon appointment cards create a small paper mountain spotted with coffee stains. I take a tenner. She's so careless with money, she won't miss it, and even if she does, she'll think she spent it on something she's already forgotten. I check the time on the cooker. Mac will be home from work soon and he'll get aggy because the sink is piled up with dirty dishes, and the vacuum cleaner is still outside my bedroom, unused, because I haven't picked the dirty laundry up off my bedroom floor.

They're talking about football now.

I'm wearing Mum's khaki playsuit and her new gold belt, so I need to sneak out before she notices, or she'll make me change. It's not like she's going anywhere tonight. Mac will come home, they'll choose a takeaway, probably pizza with garlic bread as we had a chippie last night, and then they'll huddle up on the sofa with a couple of cans of lager and a couple of episodes of *The Walking Dead* which she'll talk all the way through. I tuck the tenner inside the top of the playsuit with my phone, dash to the front door, and yell, "I'm going out with Cee!" as I close it behind me.

"Summer!" Mum calls but I pretend I didn't hear her.

Cee is already waiting outside. She lives two doors along from me. It's not a street exactly, more a raised walkway reached by a flight of steps at one end or a spiral ramp at the other. The whole estate is a maze of pathways; flats join onto houses, and houses join on to flats like a concrete 3D jigsaw puzzle with the woods framing two sides. Which is the only thing the place has going for it. Foxes come in to explore the concrete at night, tipping over rubbish bins and leaving a mess behind, swapping places with the kids who migrate to the woods or the park with some alcohol or anything else they can pick up without getting caught.

Cee's real name is Courtney—which she hates—so her friends call her Cee for short. I wave the tenner at her. She shakes her head and laughs.

"We'll save it for later. Ritchie's already got booze."

My stomach somersaults and I fix the smile to my face so that Cee doesn't notice while I wait for it to settle. Cee's brother Ritchie is three years older than us. They have different dads and Ritchie is a lot darker than Cee, and even though he'll have his arms around another girl when we get to the park, I still won't be able to stop my legs from shaking whenever I look at him.

We meet at the park most evenings now the weather has warmed up and it's not raining all the time. There's a crowd of us. The others are mostly older, Ritchie's age, which means they can bring booze and fags and anything else that's going. Cee has always seemed more their age, which means Ritchie is happy for her to tag along, and I'm there by association. Even though we play music, the neighbours never complain about us; it's not like we destroy the place and terrorise little kids or anything. We're just hanging out. Minding our own business. Getting pissed mostly.

Cee is quiet tonight while we walk to the park, cutting through the estate and then crossing the main road which divides the two sides of town: the rat-warren where the kids play hide-and-seek in the alleyways, and the big houses with BMWs parked on the drives and hot tubs in the back gardens.

I'm not paying attention because some guy I met in a nightclub has popped up on my Snapchat. We're not old enough to get into clubs, but we've all got fake IDs and because we hang around with people who are older than us, the bouncers let us in, no questions. That, and because we always make sure they can see a nipple.

"You remember that guy from the Venue who said he was a barber?" I ask.

"What? Who?"

"The flash geezer with the Audi. The night we stopped for kebabs and then you spewed everywhere."

"Oh, yeah, vaguely," she says.

Cee gets like this sometimes. Most days, our messages are like a running commentary of our lives.

My mum's in the bathroom and I need to pee.

Ritchie just burped in my face. He's so gross, I don't know what girls see in him.

I'm watching Hunted. We should apply as soon as we're old enough. We'll be hilarious.

And then sometimes I don't hear from her all day, and I sit at home stressing that I've done something to upset her, guzzling Diet Cokes and pigging out on popcorn, and arguing with Mum when I'm too full to eat dinner. But, later in the evening, I'll creep upstairs to the tiny room at the top of our house where the window opens onto the V-shaped roof, and she'll be on her roof with her cuddly bunny, and we'll both listen to Drake through our earbuds at the same time.

I patch the Snapchat for now and link my arm through hers.

Everyone is buzzing when we reach the park. I love it when it's like this. Ritchie's mates dancing on the grass, a couple of boys kicking a ball about, and me and Cee. I feel like no one can touch us, like we can do whatever we want because we're young and special and immortal. And that's before I have a beer.

Ritchie doesn't have a girl joined to his hip tonight. He brings us a couple of cans and drapes an arm over each of our shoulders from behind, kissing the tops of our heads.

"How's my two favourite girls?" he asks.

Cee shoves him away. "You've been eating Peperamis; you stink."

Ritchie chases her and she runs from him screaming until he catches her and swings her around, his arms around her waist and her feet flying above the ground. She struggles to get free, and he cups his hands around her face, breathing over her. I join in with the laughter. I wish he would do that to me, but it's like there's this big invisible barrier between us since the time we kissed.

Still, Cee is smiling now, and I feel a pang of guilt that I didn't ask what was wrong before we got here.

Once the last few little kids and their mums clear out of the play area, we all pile in. The boys claim the climbing frame that's built to resemble a castle, sitting at the top, some of them swinging upside down from the monkey bars. Cee and I take over the swings. Ritchie pushes us like he's our dad, and we swing higher and higher until the whole frame is vibrating with the movement.

My hair is in my face and I'm starting to feel sick when a little boy appears in front of us like an apparition. He is wearing shorts and a stained T-shirt, and his face is grubby as though he has been crying and has rubbed the tears away with dirty fingers.

"What the hell?" Cee says. "Ritchie, stop! I need to get off."

Ritchie grabs the chains holding up Cee's swing and she almost falls off with the force of it. I'm sitting upright on my swing, waiting for it to slow. I don't even feel like I've had a beer now.

Cee jumps off the swing while it's still juddering about. "Vinny, what the fuck are you doing here?" She grabs the boy by his skinny arm and starts dragging him towards home, yelling at him about crossing main roads and bedtime.

Sometimes, I forget that her brother Vinny exists. Cee is always looking after her two youngest siblings, but Vinny seems to live outside with a bunch of other kids his age, occasionally popping into the house for food and drink. As they walk away, Cee doesn't glance backwards.

I stay a while. Someone offers me vodka from a water bottle which he pours into my can of beer. Ritchie wanders off to sit on the grass. I swing lazily back and forth, my trainers scuffing the bark underfoot, my arms turning rusty brown from the chains. I don't know how long Cee has been gone because I forgot to check my phone when she left, but it feels like ages.

I'm about to join Ritchie on the grass when I look up and there's a girl sitting beside him. She's skinny, dark-skinned, pretty, with red lipstick. I watch as she leans closer, her long black hair forming a veil around them like they're hiding behind a curtain or something and kisses him. I don't know if she is deliberately moving slowly to make sure everyone is watching or whether my brain has activated slow-mo, but either way, my eyes are glued to them.

My phone dings and I almost drop my can of beer and vodka. It's Mum.

I ordered you pizza.

I instinctively message back:

I'm not hungry.

I can't think about food right now. Every time I see Ritchie with a new girl, I tell myself that it won't last, that he's messing around because that's what boys do, that it's only a matter of time before he looks at me the same way.

I down my drink. The fuzzy feeling inside my head makes it easier to deal with. I get up off the swing, trip over a small rock, and glance around to see if anyone has noticed, but the boys are all too busy laughing and climbing and having a kickabout. I don't even know if Cee is coming back. I send her a message:

Where are you?

No reply.

As I walk towards the woods at the top of the hill to take the shortcut home, one of Ritchie's mates yells, "Where are you going?"

"Home!" I shout over my shoulder. I don't look at Ritchie and hair-girl. He probably hasn't even noticed me leaving and that will hurt even more.

2

The woods begin at the crest of the hill as though the slope is a face, and the trees are a quiff. I could walk the raggedy path with my eyes closed; all the kids know their way around the woods. When I was younger, I had this creature, a bear-wolf, who lived in a hollow by the tree with snake-roots—she looked after my trinkets which were shiny things I stole from Mum and Gran: beads, a loose gem from a bracelet, thin shiny belts. When I was with her, tucked up in the hollow where no one could see us, her heartbeat like the telly playing Disney movies in the background, I felt like I was the most loved girl in all the land.

I shake my head at the thought, but still my eyes seek out the twisted tree, and for half a beat, I consider changing direction. I still have the buzz in my veins from when we arrived at the park, only now its muted, and I don't know how to get it back.

At home, I let myself in the front door, and Mac is in the kitchen, showered, his work clothes probably in a heap on the bathroom floor splattered with paint and smothered in a fine layer of plaster-dust.

"I've left the dishes in the sink for you," he says. He smells of after-shave and shampoo. He's wearing a Tommy Hilfiger

T-shirt and jeans and is holding his tobacco tin as though he's on his way out.

"Hello, Summer," I say. "Have you had a good day?"

I get it from Mum—she lives for sarcasm.

Mac takes a deep breath. "If that's the way you want to play it, I'll stay home in the morning and drag you to school myself, because I'm betting you've been nowhere near the place dressed like that." He takes in the playsuit and I wait for it to dawn on him. Three . . . two . . . one. "Does your mum know you're wearing her clothes?"

I laugh in his face. "I'll see you in the morning, then, yeah."

I open the microwave, take out the small Margarita pizza they got me for dinner, and head down to my room. He doesn't even follow me; it's a fine line between setting some ground rules and having Mum tell him to butt out because he's not my dad. I hear the front door close behind him as I reach my room.

I kick off my boots, flop onto my bed and check my phone—still nothing from Cee. The pizza is cold and stodgy, so I pick the topping off and eat that, and leave the rest in the box. I stick *Gossip Girl* on my telly and watch a few episodes. Chuck and Blair always make me smile, because no matter how many wrong turns they take, no matter how many doomed-to-fail relationships they have with other people, I know they'll end up together. That's what's going to happen with me and Ritchie.

It's late, the world a giant dark shadow through the window, when I get another snapchat from the geezer with the Audi asking if I'm asleep. He's driving around our estate. If Cee had been here with me, I'd have probably patched it again, but I'm bored, and the vodka has worn off, so I tell him to give me five and I'll be outside.

I sneak upstairs to the top floor, the house shadowy and silent, and climb out of the window and across the roof to get out. It's safe; all the kids do it. The houses are built so that, although this room is upstairs, the rest of the house is ground level and lower, and the window opens on to a safe slanted roof that follows the houses to the end of the row, where it's a low drop onto the grassy slope, and down to the garages. All the kids use the roofs to smoke. No one takes any notice if they see someone sitting out there with a bottle, or a packet of fags, or clambering along to jump off the other end. The architects who created this estate won awards for the space-saving design, apparently. I bet they were off their tits at the time.

I can hear music thumping from inside his car. It sounds like a party.

I don't know much about this guy, Tom. He's older than me, good looking in a slick, clean way, like his mum probably still irons his shirts and polishes his shoes, but it's okay because one of our friends knows his sister. I think I told him I was eighteen when I met him in the club, and he didn't question it. I'm hoping he's got some alcohol in the car. It'll be better chat if I've had a drink.

He flashes his headlamps at me when he sees me coming. I'm about to open the passenger door when I realise there's another guy in the car with him, so I climb on to the back seat.

Tom smiles at me from over his shoulder. "Alright, sweetheart? Looking sexy."

The other guy eyes me up and down and tells me his name

is Adam. I think. I mean, the music is banging and it's warm inside the car, and I already feel like my cheeks are on fire.

"Did you get out okay?" Tom asks. "No problems?"

I shake my head. "Have you got any drink?"

He nods at his mate who hands me a hip flask. I take a long swig and it's like drinking fire, warming me as it travels down my body.

"I thought you was bringing your mate?" Tom asks.

I shrug. "She went home early."

"It's okay the three of us," says the guy in the passenger seat. He takes back the hip flask and brings it to his lips, his eyes never leaving mine.

This isn't the way I pictured it. I thought Tom was going to take me for a drive around town, show off his flash car, listen to some banging tunes, maybe have a kiss when he dropped me back home, but this feels different.

I consider telling them I've changed my mind, getting out of the car, and going back home to bed, but I'm not tired, and I don't want to be awake in the morning if Mac decides to follow through with his threat. Instead, I find Cee on Messenger and hit the green button. She takes a while to pick up and I can tell I've woken her up.

"Summer?"

"Cee!" I say. "Come out. I'm with Tom, we're parked at the end of the street."

"Who?" Her voice is thick with sleep.

"The guy I was telling you about earlier."

"I dunno," she says. "I dunno if I can be arsed."

"Please." I turn to the side window so that they can't see my face from the front seats. "Bring some drink if you've got

16

some. It'll be fun." I sense the hesitation at the other end of the phone and picture Cee in her pyjamas, her bunny tucked under the duvet with her. "Please, Cee, I had a row with Mac, I don't want to go home yet."

I breathe on to the glass and watch it mist up, staring beyond it at the grubby brick houses. I don't want to be stuck inside. I want to get pissed so that everything goes away and when I wake up tomorrow morning, I can start afresh with no memory of tonight.

"Okay, where are you?"

"Come across the roof and you'll see us."

I notice a look pass between Tom and his mate, and I ignore it.

Ten minutes later, Cee is running towards the car, a plastic bottle in her hand, her hair in a ponytail that swings from side to side behind her.

"You're crazy," she says, closing the rear door behind her. She's breathing heavily and smiling, and already it feels as though someone has opened the roof and allowed the fresh air in. Cee has that effect on people and situations. When she's on form, she's the North star, shining brightly so I can see where I'm going. And when she's down, I'm down too. She hands me the bottle. "I was going to bring this to the park but then I got stuck doing bath-time with the kids."

I swallow a mouthful of gin and hand it back to her.

"So, where are we going?" she asks.

"Let's drive and see where we end up," Tom says. He turns the music up louder and puts the car into gear.

As we head down the hill and away from the estate, Cee leans closer and opens her hand, gesturing with a tilt of her head for me to look. She brought pills. We take one each and wash it down with gin.

I feel the music vibrating in my chest, and around my skull, and we're singing along, smiling at each other as though we're doing karaoke on a Thursday night at the Charlatan where all the old men hang out. We drain the bottle after a few songs. The music is so loud, and my head so fuzzy, everything blurs around the edges so that when we sing, it feels like we're on the radio. Bright new stars.

It's dark, and there are no streetlamps, so I have no idea where we are, but I'm riding with the buzz.

"Faster!" I shout.

Cee laughs out loud. "Go faster!"

The song changes to Drake singing 'God's Plan.'

"Turn it up, this is my favourite song," Cee says.

The rear-view mirror is vibrating with the beat, and my chest is vibrating too. "Can you feel it?" I ask Cee.

"What?" She's shouting to be heard.

"Can you feel it?"

The car slows, turning off the road, but it doesn't matter. We can have a party wherever we are.

I'm holding my hands to my chest, showing her that I can feel the music rattling my ribs when the sound of metal hitting something solid obliterates Drake's voice and everything lurches forward. Her face changes, registers something going on inside that I don't understand, her eyes wide and lips slack, and I'm left with an echo of 'God's Plan' bouncing around inside my head.

3

Mum leans against the bed, my drip tubes rolling beneath her hips. She reaches for my hair extensions, twirls them around her finger and drapes them across my shoulder as if, any minute now, a camera crew will bustle through the door and she'll give me the side-eye and say, "Smile."

It'll be better for everyone if I look innocent.

They talk amongst themselves. Gran rolling her eyes at Grandad because he's reading the newspaper instead of giving me sympathy, and Mac checking out social media on his phone. Mum mentions Tia's wedding, how we can all look forward to seeing me in my bridesmaid dress, baby pink and floaty, fifties style.

"She'll look like Audrey Hepburn with her hair up," she says.

I look nothing like Audrey Hepburn, hair up or down.

"There, Summer, you see," Gran says. "All this to look forward to still." She hesitates, her brain cells fumbling over insensitive words, and settles on, "Stay strong, baby girl." Her hand reaches across the bed half-heartedly, ending up on the washed-to-death thermal blanket somewhere close to my knee.

When the nurse comes in and eyes us up, nodding at the

sign on the wall that says TWO VISITORS PER BED, they shift in their plastic seats and Mum snatches my hand into both of hers claiming her right to be there.

"I can let you stay a bit longer if you're quiet," the nurse says. Her name badge says Marina. She's short, shorter than me, and pretty, and that's with no foundation or contouring, and natural brows. I wonder if she's had her lips done though. "How are we doing?"

"She's doing really well," Mum says, squeezing my fingers. "Looks like a ghost though, could do with some colour in her cheeks."

Marina keeps her eyes on the equipment. "I just need to do your observations. Slide a finger in here and I'll take your blood pressure while we wait."

As the wrap tightens around my arm, I close my eyes and wait for my head to explode.

I didn't pay attention when they spoke about concussion and whiplash, when they mentioned dizziness and fainting, when they x-rayed my ribs and fitted the collar, when they checked behind my eyes with their tiny blinding light. Mum's fingers trembled on my arm from lack of nicotine, her smile persistently wringing out.

"I'm so proud of you," for the doctors' benefit. "You're so strong, baby," and, "You've got this."

She has a list of them picked up from the soaps and her pals the Kardashians, her own peculiar brand of reality in which Mum and Baby Girl wow their followers with their tiny lives. I didn't pay attention because my brain was playing Drake's 'God's Plan' on repeat. I came up for air, gulped in the smell of antiseptic, the bite of bleach, the sterile mauve of an alien room in which people spoke in library-whispers and rubbed my arms like they were warming me up and I closed my eyes again.

"All done." Marina unwraps me, my head still intact. "Ten minutes, guys."

They hover.

"Your clothes are in here." Mum points to the flaky metal cabinet beside the bed. "Get some rest and we'll be back in the morning."

"Try not to worry," Gran says.

"They've given her something to help her sleep," Grandad says. "She'll be fine."

In the end Mac steps in with a wink in my direction which no one else notices.

"I think we should go," he says. "It's been a long night." He stands and they follow his lead.

Mum strokes my hair away from my forehead and kisses the top of my head. Gran squeezes my arm. Grandad salutes me from the end of the bed.

I close my eyes until they're gone, footsteps and whispers receding through a tunnel.

The drip tube tugs out easily. Yanking off the collar, I slide my legs over the side of the bed and ease my weight on to my feet. My legs are shaky, but I can stand. It takes a while to drag on my boots, my head incapable of leaning forward without lurching me sideways and making me gag, so I've finished half a jug of lukewarm water by the time I've slid my dress over my hospital gown. Mum's black denim jacket is on the back of the chair and I slip that on to cover my hospital wristband.

My phone says 03:55. A couple of hours should be long enough.

The corridor is dimmed, hushed. The doors between here and the glow of the ward reception are all closed, no staff about. I tiptoe as far as I can and then wave over my shoulder to the desk as I hit the green button to release me. The rest is easy.

Some skinny old geezer is outside the main entrance in his pyjamas and a bobble hat smoking a fag, his drip bag on a stand beside him, fluffy wine-coloured slippers on his feet. He nods at me, at my normal clothes, blows smoke into the air. He doesn't care; he's killing his lungs anyways. As long as I leave him to get on with it, he isn't saying anything, and if I'm stopped by hospital staff, I'll tell them to go get their priorities right and drown his tobacco-stash in the loo instead of chasing me down the road, because if I was actually ill, I'd be in my bed snoring with the rest of them.

The hospital backs on to the woods, designed to bring nature inside because trees and birds help with the healing process. It saves me a bus journey. I need to head south around the town towards the river. I remember when they started building the hospital, how I'd worried about them destroying the woods because of my bear-wolf, but the land they turned into a construction site was only wasted land between the scrap merchant and the packaging company. It didn't even affect the animals who probably all crawled closer to the river to avoid the noise of the cranes and the diggers and came back when it was all over.

I know if I keep the town and the council estate to my left and cut diagonally away from the hospital towards the river, I'll get there eventually. Once I start walking my head feels less like it might topple off my neck any second, and more like if I stare straight ahead at least I won't walk into a tree. I soon get my bearings and it's like the woods, the river, and the silent invisible animals are holding their breath, expecting me. It's never dark here. Well, it's dark but the moon paints everything silver and it makes me feel like a princess. A real princess. There are fairy lights around my bed at home, around the head end and the foot end, but they're pink and tacky with two years' worth of bedroom dust, and nothing like the pure diamond stars I can see above the trees.

In the moonlight I could keep going, get as far away as possible and sleep when it's daylight, but Mum will be panicking if she gets back in the morning and I'm gone. She'll shout and holler at whoever gets in her way, she'll march along the corridors, heels clacking, and it'll be everyone else's fault that she doesn't know where I am.

I could tell them a few things. I could tell them a lot of things, but I won't because we must stick together, and my memories are still fuzzy around the edges from the pills so I can't quite tell the real ones from the dream ones.

I follow the kind-of-path with the big trees leaning towards the river-spray on my left and the dense jungle-bushes on my right; I try not to stare too hard at these in case I see red glinting eyes or hear twigs snapping, because the little-girl fear that monsters come out at night is lurking on my shoulder, and I'm not quite close enough yet to be saved.

The hollow, when I find it, seems smaller, closer to the path, too far away from the park, but that's probably because I'm taller and faster. My bear-wolf must sense me approaching because she does the crying thing that gets inside your head and behind your eyebrows, and I follow the sound like we're connected by telepathy or something. Between the trees, parting branches and avoiding nettles, I spot the entrance like a rabbit tunnel formed of spun leaves and sticks. Dropping to my knees I crawl inside curling into a tight ball with my chin on my knees. I've lost my shoes, or maybe I didn't put them on because I wiggle my toes and the soles of my feet feel cracked and sore. I'm not wearing pants either; the chill between my legs makes me shiver.

I shimmy closer to my bear-wolf and smooth her soft fur to get comfortable. She's warm, so warm it hits me like a slushy going down how freezing I am. She still has the ribbons in her hair from last time I came when I brought combs and hair gems and large floppy bows, and she sat patiently while I made her look pretty. It was like my toy styling head only better because my bear-wolf was real. She'd grinned at me when I told her my secrets and turned her head this way and that so I could tie matching plaits behind her ears, and the smell of her breath on my cheek was like jelly and ice cream, and my secret pillow all rolled into one.

Her cold nose tickles my neck. It's exposed without the collar they gave me for whiplash, and I wonder how it would feel if it snapped. I'm pretty sure nothing is broken, nothing visible anyway. She rolls on to her side, her large paws circling my body like I'm her baby and nudges my cheek so she can see into my eyes. She wants to know if it hurts. I can't tell her it doesn't hurt enough.

The sound issuing from the back of her throat is like a human cry, like she's trying to speak but it's too painful and all she can do is cry with me. Tears spill onto my cheeks because I know she understands. She feels what I feel. Without judging, she's sharing my pain.

I breathe in her feral animal smell, press my tears into her neck and concentrate on the rumbling in her chest. It's the only way I can get 'God's Plan' and Cee out of my head. It was the last song we heard in the car. The music was turned up so loud and I yelled, hoarse, at Cee, did she feel it in her chest too?

She felt it. She was laughing out loud although her face was blurry from the pills. She was wearing a Minnie Mouse vest under her *Friends* hoodie because she didn't have time to change. She came running down the slope, giggling because I'd got her out of bed, breathless with excitement. She said I was crazy. The music blared louder. She laughed and sang along until the sound of metal on wood drowned out the tune and twisted my heart in my chest. Her head snapped forward in slow motion, shock registering in her eyes, her hair smothering her face, the seat belt pinning her back. She stopped singing. Her lips were still framing the lyrics as they turned blue, her eyes still shining like she was having the time of her life.

The silence was the giveaway.

4

Fifty Shades of Grey is on the telly. We've worked our way through *The Little Mermaid*, *Frozen*, *Deadpool*, and *Walking on Sunshine*. Mum said she'd saved the best for last. She's back on the exercise bike while she waits for Mac to come home from work, soggy patches spreading across her vest, and damp tendrils of witchy hair clinging to her creased forehead.

I try not to look at her. I try not to breathe in the perfume that wafts from her skin, or the anticipation of Mac's homecoming that settles on our shoulders like the gloomy drizzle outside the windows. I bury myself deeper into the duvet bunched up around me like soft cloud, and stare at the photos on my phone. Cee's face pouts back at me. She wanted lip-fillers, begged Ritchie to pay for them when he started work at the pâté factory, but studying her features now, I can't understand why. She was beautiful. She had a natural healthy glow, wide eyes, strong thick hair that was straight out of a magazine even when she'd rolled out of bed after a night on the piss, and lips I'd have died for when she smothered them in lip gloss.

I should feel guilty thinking I'd have died for her lips when Cee is the one who died, but I don't.

She knows what I mean.

She knew what I meant.

She got me.

Right now, I'd die to have her back, even if in all our pictures I resemble a skinny ghost painted up like a china doll beside her.

There'll be an inquest. We weren't even travelling fast; Tom didn't see the fencepost because there were no streetlamps. We got whiplash and Tom had a suspected cracked rib from the airbag inflating. I still don't understand why Cee had to die, I mean, I took the same pills and I'm still here. How is this fair?

I select some photos to post on Facebook. In most of them my roots need doing, and my nails are rubbish, not like Mum's sparkly pink ones with crystals on the second finger, but you can see we're besties and that's what counts. My favourites are the ones taken on Cee's sixteenth birthday at the Tavern. Everyone was there: me, Cee, Frankie, Tia. We were knocking back Tia's Tequila before we went out, but the music was banging, and I remember Cee said it was the best night of her life because she was with me.

I start typing a status about how much fun we had that night, and for a moment I almost forget that she won't read it, that she'll never suggest another night out—she's gone. I glance at Mum sweating her tits off on her bike when she should be resting, and I feel like I'm buried alive in this house. In this duvet. In this life.

Mum called the school and told them I needed time to heal. God knows why she bothered; they haven't seen me in months. Now, even the loss of school with the gangs of girls huddled over their phones and their navy acrylics, and the boys always poking and punching and dicking about, is making me feel claustrophobic.

I miss her so much.

I delete what I've written and type:

Miss you baby girl xxx

And post it along with the images even if it does make me sound like my mum. In the front door, a key turns and Gran calls out, "Only me," like we don't expect to see her every afternoon. I smell her SJP perfume as she bustles about in the kitchen, a carrier bag being crumpled and stuffed into the cupboard under the sink, the top cupboard opening and closing as she stocks the shelves with chocolate digestives and Kenco latte sachets. She doesn't drink Nescafe, and the smell of tea reminds her that Grandad is waiting at home for her to put the dinner on and fill the kettle.

"How's my baby girl doing?" She comes into the living room, leans over me, and squeezes my cheeks. I wish she wouldn't do that; it fucking hurts. "You've got a bit of colour back today, hasn't she, Lizzie?"

Mum mops her forehead with the back of her arm and nods.

Gran flops into the armchair with a *Glamour* magazine and says, "I hope you've been eating. You need to keep your strength up, you know, get back on the mend."

They need to make their minds up. Don't keep telling me how strong I am, and how proud they are of me for surviving such a tragedy, and in the next breath tell me to eat, eat, eat, because my skin is transparent, and no one likes a stick insect. Well, Mac likes my mum.

I check my phone. My Facebook status already has three likes. Tia and Frankie have both commented:

Love you forever, girl xxx

Their cousin Liam has posted three hearts. They know my heart is shattered. I'm like the tin man in *The Wizard of Oz*, an empty casing devoid of emotions and life and love. I wish I'd used that as my status—it would've got hundreds of likes.

Gran is still talking. "You know the old bastard sold my car to Shilling-Sean from up the road." She always refers to Grandad as 'the old bastard' and normally it makes me smile. But today I flinch at the mental image of him reading the newspaper at their dining table and peeking over the top of the pages at me, saying, "You still here?" but loving the company anyway, loving that I'll sit with him and watch old *Carry On* films, and laugh out loud at the predictable smutty jokes, and not roll my eyes once. Today, I wish she would leave him be.

"Yeah." Mum sits back on the saddle, downs half a pint of water without breathing.

"I told him, I did; I warned him my car weren't driving for anyone else. And you know what happened? On the way to Sean's, it had a blow-out. And this morning it won't start. 'You're an old witch,' he says to me this morning. Forty years and he's only just working it out." Her laugh rattles until she coughs.

The pedals start rotating again. "I could've told him you're a witch. Remember the bingo, Mum? You knew you was going to win and the shop. No one else would've seen that coming."

"Shame I can't predict the old bastard halfway around the

world and out of my hair." Her gold bangles jangle on her wrist as she turns the pages of the magazine. "I love this outfit but not on her." She spreads the pages and holds them up for us to view a selection of glossy Taylor Swift photographs.

The front door opens a second time. It's Mac. He removes his trainers on the mat in the hallway. Mum wipes her face with a hand towel and fixes a smile in place.

"Alright?" He pokes his head around the doorway to the living room, glances at each of us in turn. "How's my baby?"

He doesn't mean me.

"He's asleep," Mum says, although it isn't obvious how she knows this because Jonah is in his Moses basket downstairs in their bedroom.

"He's so quiet you hardly know he's there," adds Gran. "Shall I get him up?"

"No, you stay there," Mac says. "I'll get him." He gives me a look as he turns away that says he expected at least one of us to go check on him instead of lounging under a duvet all day.

We hear his gentle baby-voice as he lifts Jonah from the Moses basket. "Whoa there, little boy, who needs a clean nappy then, eh?"

"Ah he dotes on him, Lizzie. It's so lovely to see," Gran says.

Mum folds away the bike, stores it in the corner of the room behind the table and next to the messy cupboard. It's barely upright before she's reaching for the cigarettes on the windowsill and slipping her feet out of the trainers she wears for her work-out and into a pair of sparkly flip-flops. "Stick the kettle on, Summer," she says.

"I don't want a drink." I don't glance up at her. Someone else has posted some pictures of Cee on Instagram.

"I'll do it, love," Gran says sitting forward in her seat. "Meant to say—" She perches on the edge of the cushion. "The bloody mother is being interviewed by the *Echo*."

She says '*bloody mother*' like the person being discussed isn't worthy of a name, frames it in apostrophes like a toxic thing to be spat out before the rest of us are also tainted. I know who she means. She's talking about Cee's mum. She's talking as though she's the last person in the world entitled to an opinion on her own daughter's death. I mean, Cee's mum is scary, and right now she's the last person I'd want to speak to about what happened, but better the papers print her story than mine.

Cee called her mum the Ovary because she always seemed to be pregnant. I remember when she told me about the nickname.

"Have you seen her babies?" she asked.

I said that I'd seen Cee with them, and she tipped her head back to face the sky.

"Thank you!" she said. "Have you seen my mother with them?"

I had to think about it. I'd seen Cee's mum when she poked her head outside their front door to shout at her, or when my mum pointed her out and said, "Look at the size of that arse! What do men see in that?" But I wasn't sure I'd seen her with the babies.

"The answer is no. You haven't," Cee said. "You haven't seen her with them because she doesn't do anything with them. I do."

5

"They should interview Summer," Mum says now, projecting a mouthful of smoke towards the clouds and waving it away from the patio doors.

"You can bet your life she'll be painting a pretty picture of domestic bliss, no mention of the meals you gave her kid, and the nights she spent here with Summer avoiding her mother's fist. Bloody wrong, it is," Gran says.

"We can't say anything yet, but wait till after the funeral. Everyone knows how close Courtney and Summer were anyway. We don't need a story in the newspaper to prove that we cared about her. If her daughter had heart problems, why didn't she warn her about getting sloshed and taking pills?" Mum asks.

Mac appears in the doorway, Jonah held tight against his chest, a pink patch on the back of the baby's head where he's been sleeping. His downy hair is fair and wispy like dandelion fluff. I breathe in the clean milky smell of the baby, his freshly laundered sleepsuit that's been washed along with our clothes and dried on the radiator, yet still smells like tree-breath. It must be a baby-phenomenon. He wriggles in Mac's arms, rubs his forehead against Mac's T-shirt.

"I'll make you a cuppa." Gran rises and her bangles clatter

down to her elbow. She strokes Jonah's hair as she passes, says, "He's a good boy," and plants a kiss on the top of his head, barely missing Mac's chest.

Mac waits for her to leave the room. "What was your mum saying?" he asks.

She widens her eyes at him and shakes her head like I won't notice, like it's okay for her and Gran to slag off Cee's mum, but if Mac gets involved, they might have to acknowledge the fact that Cee is dead because she was out with me.

"We can talk about this you know." He jigs the baby from side to side, the baby-blue blanket flapping against his jeans. "You never know it might even do her some good to discuss what happened."

"Oh, cos you're an expert in psychology now." She flicks the butt down into the yard at the bottom of the house. The back garden, like the house, is on three levels. The bedrooms on the lower level open out onto the yard which is paved with cracked slabs and lined with niggly weeds, corners piled high with mini mountains of cigarette ends and soggy leaves. A redundant broom props up the shed, the brush a home for spiders the size of hedgehogs.

"Well, for what it's worth, I've been thinking about it and I don't think you should go to the funeral. Either of you," Mac says.

"What the fuck?" Mum steps back inside, eyes up the baby like she's unsure how he came to be here.

"Hear me out. I just think it's unfair on the family. They're grieving, Liz. No amount of time will heal the pain they're feeling right now." He kisses Jonah's cheek. "And you don't want to cause a scene."

33

I think he must realise what he's said too late, because he scrunches his eyes and shuffles his feet, waiting for the backlash he knows is heading his way.

"Oh yeah, cos me and Summer are the ones causing a scene here." She swipes the air with her forefinger like she's getting ready to count off all the reasons why Mac is wrong. Again. "Like, one, her fucking mother never causes a scene. Righto. Two. Summer's done nothing wrong."

I close my eyes and wait for her to finish.

"Liz, stop," Mac interrupts her. He's on dangerous ground and it's not as if he can make it up to her the usual way right now, so it'll cost him in other ways. The price of a new pair of boots, most likely. "All I'm saying is, let them have their day."

"What about Summer's day? What about her day then?"

This is turning into one of those big brick-wall arguments. They're the worst. They're the ones that occur when Mum refuses to listen, even when she knows she's in the wrong but won't be reasonable because, once she's jumped in feet first, she can't reverse her way out of it. Mac always says the reverse gear in her car should be preserved, immaculate, in a 173

for superfluous car parts.

"I'm not saying Summer can't have her day, Liz, but think how her mum would feel with Summer there."

"What's that supposed to mean?" The kettle clicks off in the kitchen and her voice slices the air, suddenly knife sharp.

"Well . . ." He studies the top of Jonah's head for the correct answer. "Summer was there."

"And?" She's already fumbling for her next fag.

"Come on, Liz, you know what I'm saying. Did you know

where Summer was? Did you know she was out with a guy who was practically old enough to be her dad?"

I watch her eyes narrow. We both know that if she'd caught me sneaking out of the house, I'd have lied, and she wouldn't have pushed it. Easier that way. "So, what, this is Summer's fault now? The girl could've said no."

Mac meets my eyes and looks away. He knows I wouldn't have taken no for an answer if I wanted to do something, but he's trying not to start World War 3. "How would you feel if it was the other way around? If—"

"I know what the other way around means," she snaps. "I wouldn't stop the girl from coming to the funeral."

"You're sure about that are you?" Mac's voice has dropped, and his arm covers Jonah's ears, but I can feel the menace in it, the spite.

I wish I could evaporate beneath the duvet. My legs are damp with sweat, but any movement is going to draw their attention to me, so I stare at my phone and imagine I'm paddling in the sea in icy water that makes my toes tingle, and I try to make the pretend chill travel up my legs and into my chest.

"Course I'm fucking sure. They were best mates. I was practically the girl's mother because her own one didn't give a shit about her."

"Don't raise your voice in front of the baby, Liz. I didn't raise my voice to you."

"Don't raise your voice, Liz," she mimics. "You're so fucking perfect. 'Cos you're just having a regular discussion and I'm the one who's raging." She lights another cigarette, fingers shaking, and holds it outside while the rest of her body remains inside the room.

35

"Right, calm?" Mac still holds the baby's head against his chest as though he's protecting him from the thunder he knows is brewing. They've forgotten, I think, that I'm still in the room. He speaks slowly as though to a child. "Yes, they were best friends. Yes, she stayed here more than she stayed at home, but that doesn't mean her mum didn't love her. And has it not occurred to you that your fifteen-year-old daughter should not have been driving around in some pill-popping twat's car at 1am in the morning?"

And the bomb drops.

"Oh, so now you're telling me what a useless fucking mother I am?"

They're just words. She has so many of them rattling around in her empty brain she can't stop them from spilling out. I know the pattern: she'll shout until she loses her voice, talking through Mac, and over him, and over Gran when she mentions the baby shouldn't be hearing them argue; she'll repeat the same sentence, the words eternally rearranged as if they mean something different each time that she says them. And then she'll cry. Mac will pour her a glass of wine and fetch her pink pills, and in bed they'll be like animals chasing the moon. Well, maybe not this time.

Ugh!

A comment pops up on my Facebook status.

You'll stay away from Courtney's family if you know what's good for you. Call yourself a friend!

I click on the commenter's picture. I don't recognise her at first, but when I enlarge the image, it looks like the girl from the park, Ritchie's current-but-soon-to-be-ex girlfriend. Who the hell does she think she is!

Another comment appears while I'm staring at her picture.

She'd still be here if it wasn't for you.

Beneath the duvet I'm sweating out. Even my ears are burning. I kick the cover off and try to stop the ringing in my ears and the tingling beneath my skin, but I can't think straight because the words are floating about in front of my eyes, and all I know is my thumbs are flying across the letters on my phone, and heat is swelling inside my brain.

Where was every other fucker when she needed a friend? You didn't even know her so just try and stop me. I'll be there if it's the last thing I do!

The instant I post my reply, they stop shouting. Jonah has tipped his head forward and vomited over Mum's legs.

6

"You've made me bleed." Frankie's face is horrified, eyebrows drawn together, and mouth pinched into a tight buttonhole. "Ow!" she complains again.

I'm at Tia's. Cee and Tia were friends when she lived near us and Cee would spend the day with her bunking off school and avoiding the Ovary. It just followed that when we were bunking off together, the three of us hung out. She's twenty-three but she likes hanging around with us because we look older anyways, and we already had fake ID for getting into clubs; Mum got mine from one of her mates. Throw on some false eyelashes and flirt with the bouncers and you're in anyways, especially on a Thursday or Sunday night. We were both going to be bridesmaids at her wedding this summer.

Tia sits back on the coffee table, her arse barely missing a glass of Asti, and laughs as we scream.

"What's the matter with yous? *She's* crying cos I've filed her nails." She points at Frankie who is sucking her little finger. "And I didn't spill the drink, did I?"

"You filed away half my finger," Frankie says.

"I file Bliss's nails harder than I did yours, you wuss." She downs a glass of wine and tops it up from a bottle on the floor beside the sofa.

Bliss, all strawberry blonde curls, and blue eyes, waves her fingers at Tia from the crayons and colouring books spread across the carpet, and says, "Mummy, want."

"You're bloody right Mummy does want," Tia says, but she dips the glass so the child can take a sip anyway. Bliss swallows, and tears collect along her thick eyelashes as she blinks furiously. "That's my baby," laughs Tia.

"Teaching her young," Frankie says.

I wish they would shut up. *To all the Boys I've Loved Before* is on Netflix. I love this film. I love Peter Kavinsky and how cute he is with Lara Jean—shame boys aren't like that in real life; I've watched it before with Cee and imagined it were me and Ritchie in school together, and that he wrote me little notes every day. I should've stayed at home wrapped in my duvet in front of the telly because this isn't the same without Cee. I only came because Mum said I needed to stop shutting myself away and get back out there.

"Can we get this done?" I ask. I notice how Tia rolls her eyes at me and I ignore it.

Tia has makeup brushes and about fifty cosmetic bags spread across the living room floor of her flat, with a cracked iPad showing a distorted image of Rick Astley, and an almost empty bottle of peach schnapps on its side under the table. We, her bridesmaids, are helping her find the look she's after for her wedding in two months, and finalisingtravel arrangements for the hen weekend in Butlin's at Bognor.

I love her to bits, but I don't know why she's marrying Jay, other than the new kid she's growing in her belly. She's rabbiting on about getting more money out of Bliss's dad.

They're doing my head in today. It seems like they've already forgotten Cee existed, like she hasn't even left a shadow in this room.

Once, last year when the nights were getting longer, Cee asked me if I could be an animal, which one would I choose? We were on our backs on the grass at the park, watching the clouds racing in the wind, squinting, trying to make animals from cloud shapes. Cee was smoking a cigarette stolen from the Ovary. I took the occasional drag. It no longer made me cough, but still burned my throat and made my head spin.

"I'd be a snow leopard," she said, without waiting for my answer.

I opened my mouth and let the smoke out, the way I'd watched Cee do it, and handed the cigarette back to her. "Why?"

"I watched a documentary once about them. There was a mother with her cubs. The fathers don't stay with them to bring the cubs up—no surprises there." She rolled her eyes. "But she was so careful to keep the cubs hidden in the den while she hunted for food. And when she came back this one time, the cubs were gone. They lived quite close to humans, so they'd obviously been hunted. The mum stood in the snow and they showed a close-up of her face on the telly. She was so beautiful, Summer, her eyes were so pale like ice, and so sad. It made me cry."

I studied Courtney while she wasn't watching. She had a look in her eyes, distant, as though she didn't see the same world as me. I wondered if it was the snow leopard she was seeing or something else. Maybe it was a world in which snow leopards were not bound to someone else's cubs. Or a world in which fathers were the ones rearing the cubs, and not the mothers.

"I'll be extinct soon," she'd said.

"I'll remember you." I stared at the sky. I didn't know then if that were true. What if one day, when we grew old, and these moments were faded memories captured on an obsolete phone, what if we no longer remembered them? What if the photographs in our minds faded and disappeared? Would that make us extinct if no one remembered us? The clouds were too big suddenly. The sky was too large, overwhelming, the way it seems at night when you stare into the starry blue-black vastness and get giddy. I closed my eyes.

"The Ovary would be a frog," she said. "Legs open wide, depositing her spawn everywhere."

We laughed together, mates until extinct.

She never asked me which animal I would be, but I already knew the answer: I'd have been a bear-wolf.

Now, Lara Jean and Peter are in the hot tub and I'm on fire and icy cold all at once. My rant on Facebook got me so much abuse in return, I had to block the Ovary and some of Cee's cousins, because the things they were saying were making me feel sick. Ritchie's been silent. I know I should block him too, but that'd be like pushing him off a cliff or burying him underground—he'd be unreachable, and I'd always be wondering if he was okay.

A tiny red number 1 pops up on my Facebook app. Another comment.

Too scared to show your face now? You know when you're not welcome. Show your skanky lying turd-face at that funeral and we'll tell the police what really happened.

The Ovary has spread her anger like water and is tracing every tiny crack and crevice and friend of a friend to get to me. And they can't even spell 'scared'.

"You're quiet, Summer girl," Tia says reaching over and stroking my foot. "You're not still letting them get to you?"

I nod. The comment is from a guy called Paul; I've no idea who he is. Tears sting behind my eyes. I've been running on anger and sorrow and Disney princesses, but now I'm just empty. There's only one person who'd know how to make me feel better and she's not here, and the enormity of the hole she's left in my world hits me like a wrecking ball.

"They're nothing. You know Cee was happiest when she was with you. And you know her mum is all about the attention now she hasn't got someone to bring up the kids for her. She'll be trying to make some money out of it, bet your life," Tia says.

I nod again. My fingers are shaking so much I can't block this geezer, and I'm thinking about what he said, that he'll tell the police what really happened, so I'm not even paying attention. What if he tells them I made her come out with me? They'll check our phones, and they'll know I called her, and the Ovary will tell them Cee would never have been driving around with strange men in the middle of the night. It's squeezing the air from my lungs because it's true.

"You're going to the funeral next Friday, aren't you?" Tia asks.

I shrug—I need to get out of here—and then I realise what she said. "Wait, what? The funeral is on Friday?"

"Yeah." Frankie's voice is shaky, and she gives Tia the side-eye like she should've kept her mouth shut. "We'll be there."

"We're not gonna let them fuck you off," adds Tia.

But they already have. They know the date's been set, which means the inquest has probably happened. They know where the funeral is being held which means they've probably, indirectly, been invited. I know it's not like getting an invitation through the door because I think back to Uncle Mike's funeral and you don't get like real invites, but somehow, they've been told about it. And I haven't.

"... crazy none of us knew about her heart condition," Tia is still talking. "Like, she never went for check-ups or anything, did she? Did you know about it, Sum?"

"What? No, what?" I shake my head. "What heart condition?" Mum said something when she read about Cee in the paper, but I hadn't been paying attention then either.

"Apparently there was a weakness from when she was a bubba. I don't know. And the pills and alcohol tipped her over the edge." She's looking at me like I should've known this. "Would've killed her without the shock of the car crash."

I should've known this. Did Cee ever mention it? If she did, and I ignored it, then, what the fuck? I watched her swallow the pills and wash them down with gin. I made her take more . . . I think. It's blurry now, but I remember holding the bottle to her lips and giggling when it spilled down her chin. I can't look at them, any of them, and my head's spinning with Asti.

"Mac and my mum are arguing about the funeral," I say. "It's too much hassle."

"She was your mate," Tia says but she's only saying that. I can tell because her voice has shrunk.

I stand up and knock over an empty bottle. "I've gotta go."

"You okay, baby girl?" Tia asks but she doesn't try to stop me.

7

Kofi finds me near the river. I haven't seen him in so long, since we went to different secondary schools, and he carried on with street dancing classes two evenings a week. He's taller and skinnier than I remember, and his jeans have sequin stripes down the sides.

"Summer?" he says, like I've become someone else, and then, "Fuck."

I squint to keep my eyes in their sockets. Close up, I stare at him in the clouds and realise I'm on the ground. My hands sting. There's blood on them, and one knee feels swollen. After Tia's, I went straight to the woods, to my bear-wolf. I don't know how long I stayed there, curled up in a ball with her paws keeping me safe, the Asti stirring up my thoughts like a Betty Crocker cake mix, but for a few minutes, or a few hours, I forgot about Cee stretched out cold and blue on a mortuary slab somewhere.

Kofi helps me stand, brushes dirt and leaves off my shorts. He walks me to the shop near our estate, holding my hand like we're boyfriend and girlfriend, and buys me a bottle of water. I think I keep telling him I've forgotten something, something important, like my bag or my phone. Or my best friend.

"Cee," I tell him. "She was my best friend."

"Fuck," he says again, when I drop his hand and melt into a puddle on the pavement. "Come on, up you get." Hands locked around my waist he hoists me back onto my feet. "There's a good girl. You gonna tell me what you've done?"

I giggle at this, but the giggle sticks in my throat with the memory of what happened.

What was she wearing? A hoodie. Pyjamas. Did she forget her phone? They won't stick, the images in my mind won't sit still, but I need to get them straight because if I don't, this world will stop spinning and I'll go hurtling off into outer space. Maybe that's where I'll find her.

"It's okay. It's okay, I got you."

It hurts. It hurts so much.

I'm sick in the toilet when we get home and I hear him speaking to Mum, vague words like grieving and depression and bouncing back, while she says, "She's strong. We'll get her through it." Like I've got a cold and she's stocking up on Vicks and man-sized tissues. "Loving your jeans by the way."

He slips off my shoes and covers me with the duvet on the sofa, and while I curl up like a puppy, shivering, he brings Jonah to say hello.

Kofi says, "Hello, sis," in a cute puppet voice like he's pretending it's the baby speaking, and the pale white of the baby's head against his dark toasty muscles is the most adorable thing I've ever seen.

I smile at them and give the baby my pinkie to hold. Something inside my chest twists, the way it used to twist when I was with my bear-wolf, and for the first time my baby brother feels like he might just have been sent to keep me alive.

Shortly before my fifteenth birthday, Cee was posing in front of my full-length mirror. Her hair, mussed up by bending forward and scrunching with both hands before rubbing the tangles with my duvet, was like the sticky layer of weeds covering the flower bed at the back of our garden. She'd stuffed a pillow inside her top before flopping backwards onto my bean bag, neckline pulled low.

"I need some fags, Court," she whined, hands dangling above the floor. "The baby needs changing, Court. Why should I have to do everything?"

We both giggled until our cheeks ached. Earlier she'd exaggerated her lips with baby-pink lipstick, drawn on panda-eyes with thick black eye liner, and stood against the wall with one knee raised and one arm above her head. Lily Fisher, a girl from our year at school who said her mum was saving up to get her a boob job when she was sixteen.

She composed herself, took a deep breath. "Get this baby out of me, Court," she said in a dramatically breathy voice.

I leaped off the bed, slid the pillow out from under her top and sat back down with it propped on my knees and pretended to feed it a bottle of milk.

"I don't know what's so difficult," I said. "Come on, baby, give me a burp."

Cee, laughing, jumped up, grabbed a plump pink sequinned cushion, and threw it at me. I ducked and the cushion hit the bedroom door.

I sucked in my breath. "Look what Mummy Courtney's done," I said to the pillow on my lap. "Bad Mummy."

She flopped onto the bed beside me and stared at the ceiling. "You're so lucky your mum is different," she said.

I replaced the pillow. "Why does she make you look after them?"

"Because she's a lazy fucking bitch. At least your mum's ovaries are sealed tight. I'm never having babies when I'm older. I'm getting a career, and taking my holidays in Bora Bora, and wearing nothing but designer outfits."

"You should own a mini-pig."

"A mini-pig?"

"Yeah, you can carry it around in your designer handbag like a chihuahua. All the posh people own one. I've seen them in magazines."

"You can be such a dumb-arse sometimes, Summer. You think pictures in magazines are real life." She picked away at her chipped yellow nail polish. "It's all pretend. Even rich people aren't happy."

I wanted to ask her about Ritchie, but there was never a right time because Cee hopped from one train of thought to the next: from babies to Primark to the twins from year 11, whose mum was in a wheelchair and whose dad was shagging the woman who came in to help care for his wife. When she wasn't hopping, she was quiet, and it didn't feel right to disturb her. I wanted to ask her about Ritchie and his girlfriend, but I was scared to ask at the same time. Ritchie was seeing a girl from year 11, which meant maybe he'd notice *me* next time we tagged along at the park; she was only one year older than me. And *I* had Cee.

"Come on, your turn," she said.

"My turn what?"

"To do an impression of your mum," she nodded towards the jumble of lipsticks and blushers and eye shadows spread across the dressing table surface. "I've done the Ovary," she encouraged when I hesitated.

I left the bed and sat at the dressing table. I didn't know where to start. "Don't watch," I said. "I can't do it if you're watching."

"Okay, I'm reading your *Scandal* magazine."

The magazine was my mum's. I'd snatched it from a pile on the coffee table and hidden it, along with a silver bag and a pink belt, beneath my bed.

Staring at my reflection, I smoothed red lipstick across my lips. I looked nothing like her, my lips were fleshier, my face fuller than hers which wasn't difficult, my bleached hair reflecting off my pale skin and freckles. I found a tissue in the top drawer, wiped away the colour and started again, but this time only touching the inside of my lips, keeping the lines as thin as possible. Better. I opened a purple eye shadow container and smudged powder beneath my eyes then added three coats of mascara, so my lashes were all clogged and lumpy. I peeked in the mirror at Cee face down on the bed engrossed in glossy magazine pictures of nearly naked celebs.

I needed a wig. Something ratty. I remembered the witch outfit Gran bought me one Halloween to wear trick-or-treating: a green shiny dress, more Little Mix than witch, a pointed hat, crushed velvet cloak and a black wig. I found the wig, tangled, and matted, in the bottom drawer of the wardrobe, nylon strands clinging with static to the abandoned tights and too-small bras I'd chucked in there as I outgrew them. The flesh-coloured cap still fitted though. I straightened the wig-hair around my face as best I could, and sucked my cheeks in.

"Ta-dah," I said in a pinched voice.

Cee sat up as the bedroom door opened.

Mac stood in the doorway. "Wrong time of year, girls," he said when he spotted the wig and makeup. I yanked it from my head and hid it behind my back. "Halloween come early?" He grinned.

"Just trying out our new look." Cee had an answer for everything; I wondered if she learned that from the Ovary. "We're thinking of turning Goth."

He glanced from Cee to me and back again. "Your mum won't like that, her little girl looking like a dead witch."

I glanced wide-eyed at Cee who sniggered, quickly smothering the sound with a fake cough. I stared at the floor and rubbed my eyes.

Mum appeared in the doorway and Mac snaked an arm around her neck, kissed the top of her head. They were always touchy-feely, but this wasn't their normal kind of affection; this was a tender, surreal, movie-scene kind of gesture and it made me feel hot and uncomfortable inside, in a way that their sex noises never did.

"Are you telling her, or shall I?" he said, his lips close to her head. He breathed in the smell of her. I stopped rubbing my face.

Mum stared at me without smiling. "We're going to have a baby," she said.

8

The exercise bike sits in the corner of the living room beside the Moses basket. I watch Mum's stomach flattening, becoming concave, see her cheeks sucking in with each cigarette breath, and the way she dances in her short skirts, music turned up banging-loud, and fingers pointed toward the ceiling like the bass-thump is all that exists for her. If there was a fire, Mum would save the exercise bike first.

Mac's parents stop announcing their visits and turn up whenever they're passing by, which makes no sense as they live on the other side of town where the houses have names, and the BMWs are personalised. This estate would never have entered their peripheral vision were it not for Jonah.

They're tall and thin like stringy saplings that might bend in a strong breeze, and not how grandparents should be, not soft and cuddly, smiley and filled with cupcakes and elbow-digs. Marian wears long skirts, flat brown leather sandals and no makeup; I don't have to glance at Mum's distant eyes to know what she thinks about that. Her face is long and thin too, like her hair. David is straight, upright, brittle. His moustache curls upwards either side of his mouth and I wonder if he plays with it in bed, twirling it around his fingers to get his wife excited. They smell of patchouli. It makes me gag.

In the living room the three of them, Marian, David, and Mac, perch on the edge of the sofa and the armchair, as if sitting back would spoil their clothes. Mac doesn't lounge with his legs slung over the sofa arm; he sits forward knees spread wide, arms resting on his thighs, and rubs his thumb around and around the rim of his coffee mug. He doesn't smoke. He doesn't roll a joint. He looks nervous somehow.

Marian has this peculiar way of fluttering her eyelids when she speaks so that only the whites of her eyes can be seen. Zombie eyes. No one else seems to notice, but I'm obsessed with them, like one day she'll take a chunk out of my neck, and I'll be a zombie too. But with Jonah she's a babe. She cradles him on her lap even while he sleeps, literally coos like a dove, "There, there. There, there, baby." David sits beside Marian on the sofa. They own the baby.

Tia isn't like this with Bliss. I remember when Bliss was born and she was passed around us like a spliff, all of us taking a baby-drag in Tia's living room, jealous because she'd had the best baby shower complete with pink and ivory flower-wall and afternoon tea, and she'd given up working in the Chinese, and had a bedroom filled with cute pink dresses and baby Kickers. Bliss wasn't labelled HANDLE WITH CARE. She wanted to stand before she could sit up unaided. She wanted to talk before she could chew lumpy food. It didn't matter if her dummy landed on the carpet, Tia would suck it and stick it straight back in her mouth.

Mac's sister Danielle is careless with her babies. Three-year-old Franco stands on tiptoes, leans on the Moses basket, and nearly topples it from the stand and Danielle smacks the back of his hand, makes him cry. He has a new sister, Milla, a fat-cheeked child with tight fuzzy curls who cries constantly and refuses to sit still in her baby chair in front of the telly. The only time she settles is when her dad picks her up. He's tall, mixed race, and so good looking I did a double take when he walked in because he looks like Ashley Banjo. Franco takes Jonah's first blue teddy and hides it in his mum's baby-bag when no one's watching. He climbs onto my lap when I sit on the end of the sofa and leans against me, thumb in his mouth. I understand how he feels.

But although our house has grown small and even more untidy, serenity has descended upon us with baby-naps and the smell of baby powder. Jonah rarely cries. He's a good boy. And his goodness must be contagious because we breathe when he's asleep, and smile when he's awake, despite the visitors.

When Grandad tags along on one of their thirty-minute visits, he follows me to the kitchen, waits for me to swig Coke from a can, says, "How are you doing, Summer love?"

"Fine." I shrug and blink furiously to scatter the scalding tears in my eyes and pray that Marian hasn't already infected me without me realising.

"How's school?" He must be embarrassed because he picks at the corners of a crinkly unrecognisable-animal painting from reception class that's still pinned to the fridge with a magnet. He knows I've not been going to school. He knows they've given up writing to my mum.

"It's still there," I say.

"How's about you come and stay with us for a while, eh? Your Gran would love it. You could help her in the shop while your mum's at home with the baby."

Ugh! It would mean meals eaten at the dining table, Grandad dripping peas and gravy onto the plate from behind his newspaper and Gran pulling faces and making snidey digs. She's only happy when he's polishing his car and yet she isn't happy when he's polishing his car. Mac reckons if Grandad didn't get such a huge pension from the police for his bad back, she'd send them photos of him playing golf and get him bollocked. Sometimes I feel sad they've swapped love for bickering, but I guess they're too stuck in their ways to change it, and I still don't want to stay with them.

"No, you're alright," I say.

Gran slips me fifty quid from Grandad's wallet when no one's watching, tells me to treat myself. She doesn't know I took a tenner from her purse when her bag was on the counter.

When they go, Mum gets in the shower and I get to watch my baby brother with his scrunched up pink face and his vague blue eyes, his tongue rolling from his mouth as if there's not enough room for it inside.

Before Mum was pregnant with Jonah, Danielle came every day with demon baby Franco. The living room was coloured with rattles, squishy rubber balls, stacking rings, and dribble. Mum and Danielle spent so many hours talking about other people, when they breathed in it was like they were settling themselves back into their own skin.

"I want to go see Gran," I said when I came home one day.

I'd been to school first period, sat through double art where Mr Thrust-my-crotch-in-your-face-if-you-sit-front-row-Talbot criticised my portrait of Kim Kardashian for being too neat, so I walked out before history. Reciting key dates from the American Civil War is never going to get me anywhere anyways.

Mum blinked at me like I was an intruder. "Gran's at the shop. And I'm busy," she said.

Baby Franco stared at me. His bottom lip rolled out; dribble trickled down his chin.

I went downstairs to listen to Drake. I heard Franco wailing even with my door closed tight, like one of those cartoon-character babies with their pink cheeks scrunched up and their mouths a wide 'O'. It was a manufactured sound, unreal.

"Summer! Come play with Franco," Mum yelled remembering I was there.

"I'm doing homework," I yelled back. I peeped up the stairs anyway.

The baby was sat on the top step looking down. He hesitated when he saw me, face frozen mid-wail, eyes wide, but when I made no attempt to climb upstairs, the bawling resumed. Louder. Redder. Hotter.

"Summer!"

I waited for them to come and scoop him up, but they didn't. Franco rocked as he screamed, bounced in his nappy precariously close to the edge of the top step. I trudged upstairs, still in my uniform, picked him up and balanced him on my hip. The crying stopped immediately leaving behind a little hiccup and jerk of his soft padded shoulders.

In the living room, music blared from the telly. Avicii. The baby twisted my hair around his little fist and pulled. "Ow," I said to him, leaning back so I could see his eyes, but he only pulled harder.

Mum glanced sideways at Danielle.

"He nearly fell down the stairs," I said, but they were talking about Danielle's neighbour whose boyfriend had just proposed with a huge diamond ring.

"Only using him for his money, she is," Danielle said.

I couldn't put the baby down. He clung to me, to my hair, my shirt, my tie which I had to remove before he strangled me. I gave him a ball—he gave it back to me. I gave him his bottle—he didn't take it. It was a while before I realised that they were whispering.

"Why don't you take him outside?" Mum suggested.

"I'll put his jumper on him," Danielle said. "He'll enjoy that."

"It'll be good practice for when Dan needs a babysitter." They winked at one another. They were like garden creepy-crawlies languishing in mud. Danielle was a large squishy slug; Mum was a wriggly worm, slipping and sliding, unfolding and stretching. Danielle had his jumper on him and the buggy ready before I could argue.

Dragging Franco's buggy over the doorstep, I went outside and closed the door, before feeling for my earphones which, I realised, I'd left on my bed. At the same time, Cee stepped outside with her sister Demi. She came straight over. "Who's this?"

"Franco. Danielle's baby."

"Demon baby?"

"Shush. They might hear you."

"I don't care." She shrugged and yelled, "DEMON BABY!" We giggled as we raced the buggies down the ramp, Demi nearly rolling over the side, and Cee catching the handles before we lost her. "That was close." She grinned.

56

At the park the grass was damp. I lifted my skirt to sit down, and I could feel wet seeping through my pants, but we couldn't be arsed to go into the play area, and besides, all the benches were taken by mums with their kids in school uniforms and their babies struggling to get out and be big boys and girls. It was better on the grass. Our own little world.

"He's kind of cute," Cee said. Franco stared at me. He wasn't interested in Demi, and she was only interested in the children on the climbing frame. She gripped the side of the buggy, twisting and turning, and curling her legs under her to see them better. Cee checked her phone and then slipped it back into her shirt pocket.

"For a boy," I said. I didn't see the cuteness despite the warm dark skin and large brown eyes. He was Danielle's baby.

"Look at his curls. He could get away with hairclips." Cee rubbed her hands through the soft wisps of Franco's hair. "Look at him."

Cee spun Demi's buggy around to face her. The baby sat back in the seat with a thump and whined because she couldn't see the park. "Shut up," Cee said. She removed Demi's soft pink fabric shoes and her frilly pink trimmed socks.

"What are you doing?" I asked.

"You'll see. Take off his shoes and socks."

"Why?"

"I want to see if he looks like a girl when he's dressed in pink." She raised her eyebrows. The wildness had gone but she was still crazy.

We swapped their shoes and socks. Franco just looked silly. Demi was a perfect tomboy in Franco's blue Kickers and grey striped socks.

"We should swap all their clothes," Cee insisted. She already had her sister out of the buggy. There was a kind of scary, smouldering energy inside Cee that I didn't dare argue with sometimes in case she self-combusted or vanished in a puff of smoke. I knew Demi and Franco weren't dolls to be dressed up for our amusement, but suddenly, caught up in Cee's moment, I really wanted to swap their clothes. I wanted to turn him into a girl while his mum bloated her pregnant belly on crisps and Coke. It was what she deserved. And I doubted the Ovary would even spot the difference if Demi was wheeled in wearing boy's clothes.

I unfastened Franco's straps and lifted him out. He touched my face as I lay him down on the grass, facing away from Demi, the tops of their heads almost touching. I removed his jumper first and then his T-shirt and shorts. He wore a vest beneath his clothes. "Are we switching vests as well?" I asked.

"No one's going to see the vests. We'll leave them on."

Franco stared at me and I couldn't fathom what he was thinking. His limbs were pliable. I was able to bend him and lift him, place the orange daisy T-shirt over his head and push his arms through the sleeves, pull the pink shorts up over his nappy without even a murmur.

When we were done, we stood back to survey our work. Demi, with her fine white-blonde curls could've been a boy with trendy long hair; grumpy, pink-faced, she tried to yank the shoes off. Franco resembled a little boy in drag. He sat there, silently watching me in his pink shorts and daisy T-shirt, as if he were waiting for applause. All he needed was a pair of stilettos and some glossy red lipstick.

"There! That'll make them take notice," Cee said.

"Are we not changing them back?" I asked. Suddenly it didn't seem like such a good idea.

"No. They expect us to look after them, they can deal with the consequences." She picked Demi up, sat her in the buggy with a thump; the baby threw the shoe on the grass narrowly missing Franco's head. I handed it back to Cee and she grabbed Demi's foot as the baby swiped at her face. "Keep the fucking shoe on," she said. The baby squirmed, her face damp and blotchy. "Wear the shoe and I'll get you a chocolate frog. You want a chocolate frog?"

It was no different to Gran saying, "Be nice to your mum and I'll buy you a phone. You want a new phone?"

9

I'm indoors, dressing up Jonah, while Cee's funeral takes place. Kofi comes around with vanilla ice cream and chocolate chip shortbread and *The Breakfast Club* on DVD, and we're spread out, the three of us, on a duvet on the floor. Mum is out. Since Jonah was born, meeting Danielle is the perfect excuse for her to leave the house and forget feed times, and wet nappies, and four-hourly routines which invariably stretch out into five- or six- or seven-hourly routines anyway, because the baby's concept of time is vague, and he never complains so we never know what he needs.

"So, you're letting them win?" she'd said as she got ready, drawing on her eyebrows.

"It's not a fight," I said. "My best mate is dead."

"I'll fucking swing for 'em if I see one of 'em," she mumbled under her breath.

After she'd gone out, Kofi said, "I see where you get it from."

He has kind hands I never noticed before. We became friends the day we started primary school because Kofi told me I'd sat in something disgusting at lunch break and said I should tie my cardigan around my waist to hide my damp skirt, and I swapped my jam sandwich for his Peperami which, he said, would make him puke if he ate it. We became inseparable. We talked too much. If the teacher asked one of us to move, the other one went too; if she asked the other one to move back, we both went. I wonder now, if we'd gone to the same senior school, would we have stayed this close? Or maybe watching me grow a pair of tits and some attitude would've pushed him away anyways, so maybe it's better this way, starting afresh, me with my acrylics and him with his skinny jeans.

Blank pages. Matching pens.

We lay either side of Jonah on the floor and take selfies of the three of us, phone held high above our faces. Angel baby, Princess, and Prince Charming. Instead of his sleepsuit, I've dressed him in grey joggers and a hoodie with *Super Baby* printed on the front; he kicks his arms and legs like he's attempting to fly, and I roll over and kiss his perfect cheek.

Against Kofi's advice, and because I can't resist, I check Tia's Instagram. There are pictures of flowers that still my heart, her status simply a broken heart, and another of Tia and Frankie dressed in black. Punishing myself, I read through the comments until I find one from the Ovary.

Lovely to see all her real friends today.

In the back of my mind, behind tiny fat fists and Johnson's baby powder and hot tears, I imagine Cee's coffin being lowered into the ground, feel the thud of dirt as it suffocates her, smothering her till the stars go out and she's become extinct. I bury my face in the duvet. If I suffocate, I can be with her again. She's the only person who gets me. No one else understands how I can't live without her. No one else understands I'm not me

61

without her. I hold my breath, press the duvet into my mouth and against my nostrils, but Kofi instinctively knows what I'm doing, and he pulls me, sobbing, from out of the cover, and wraps his thick strong arms around me, while the baby follows us with his wide blue eyes and his too-large tongue.

I expect the graveyard to be creepy, shiny white bones poking out between crackling leaves, eerie faces peeping out from behind marble headstones, ghostly noises floating on the breeze. Or inside my head. But it isn't. It isn't if you ignore the carved-out names and the body-sized mounds of grass.

Cee's grave is instantly recognisable from the gigantic floral 'C', the pink hearts, and the angel wings. The sun has followed me about since it happened, illuminating me for the world to see my guilt and my broken heart, and sucking the colour from the mountain of flowers. But still, even from the entrance, even faded, you can't miss them.

I stand in front of them suddenly self-conscious, nervous. I'm holding a white rose—I Googled it and it's supposed to symbolise spiritual love—and a copy of *The Hunger Games*, which is buckled from the heat of the radiator beneath my windowsill, because we were supposed to be together forever in the woods, learning to hunt, learning to survive. I hope if I leave it with the rose, she'll read it. Somehow.

An old woman, face crinkled and crushed, walks past me on sore feet, gold spangled jumper glinting in the sun, yellow rubber gloves and a small garden spade in her hands. She doesn't speak. I keep my head down and wait till she's passed me by before I crouch and place my offerings, like a sacrifice, on the ground at Cee's feet. It feels wrong to be standing tall while she's underground. If I think about it too hard, I can't bear the thought of her suffocating and crawling with insects, eyes crazy and nails broken and bleeding trying to dig her way out.

I glance across at the old woman bent over a grave and muttering away to herself as she tugs weeds from the soil, hoping she can't hear my panic-breathing. A quick check all around us and we're the only people here. I need to speak to Cee, but I open my mouth and the words don't come out. She's my best friend and I hate that I don't know how to speak to her when her eyes are closed and her ears can't hear anything, and she should be here telling me I'm such a twat, but she loves me anyways. I'm such a twat I can't even cry.

The old woman catches my eye and smiles. I turn away. My thighs are aching from crouching, so I kneel on the grass; it feels dry enough. A breeze ruffles the pages of the book and I read random lines as the pages spread, but they're like nonsense words rising from the mouths of the dead people I'm standing on.

"I can't even read," I say to the sky. Louder, "I'm such a twat!" The woman is still bent over, hands working steadily. "I wish you was here, Cee," I whisper. "Really here, I mean, not there." I hesitate not wanting to draw her attention to the fact she's buried inside a coffin under the ground. I need to tell her something nice. "Kofi's been round. You remember Kofi from school? Afro, wonky front tooth, made those gold pants when he played Aladdin? We've grown close. I can tell Kofi stuff but . . ." I squeeze my eyes shut. I'm conscious I'm wearing no makeup, my jeans are sagging around my arse, and the only person who would laugh about me looking a state has left me. I change the subject. "Jonah is getting chubby cheeks. I know you said I was lucky my mum was different but I'm glad he's here. I can pretend no one else exists while I'm with him. I can pretend I'm you."

I sense the woman passing behind me. She touches my shoulder and I jump because I don't want her to hear our conversation. So embarrassing. But a glance to my left and she's still there, kneeling on a kind of flat cushion and patting soil around some freshly planted primroses.

There's a spot on the mouldy-rotten balcony outside our living room that's a sun trap in the summer. From this spot I can see the rows of houses clambering up the hill behind ours, the edge of the woods to the left and a maze of houses and alleyways to the right. Leaning against the wall, earphones in, I sit on a cushion swigging gin and tonic from a can and chain-smoking cigarettes while I play one of Cee's favourite songs, 'Come and See Me' on repeat; I convince myself, in the sugar and nicotine rush, that if I can sing the lyrics all the way through without forgetting a single word, I'll open my eyes and she'll be there saying, "Get you. You've been practising."

I wish she'd get me.

I wish we could hold hands and run away together, never looking back. But even as I'm dreaming this and muddling the lyrics again on their journey between my brain cells and my tongue, I see a film set in my head with me as the tragic main character played by someone who looks like me but cries pretty, noticeable tears, not loud, snotty ones, and waits on a wooden balcony for her dead best friend to come back and get the words right.

Pathetic.

Broken.

Why did I make her come out with me that night? I want to bash the me of that day over the head with something dangerous and stop me from being such a selfish brat.

Something hard and sharp bounces off my knee. My heart panics and my eyes fly open. *Cee heard me.* That's all I can think as I glance around at the other gardens lined up in a row, a cat dozing on a golden patch of grass next door, birds chirping on a fence-top, the slope at the end of the row, close enough to the roof to jump down. She isn't there. Course she isn't there. I sit back, close my eyes again but now they're unsure, flickering, trying to catch her out.

Another tap on my shin, a pebble. My name hissed, "Summer!"

Kofi is peeping over our back fence. His aim must be spot on to have got me twice. He grins when I notice him, waves for me to come down and meet him.

Behind me in the living room, sweat flicks off Mum's hair and onto the carpet as her knees bob up and down, up and down. I slip an earphone out and listen for Jonah. Nothing. Out the back gate and Kofi is shifting his weight from foot to foot like he's cold or something.

"Come to the woods with me," he says. There's a backpack on the grass that he hoists easily onto his shoulder.

"Why didn't you knock?"

"I did," he says, facing me briefly. "There was no answer, and I thought my main man might be asleep."

It's difficult to tell but I think a bruise might be puffing up on his cheekbone. It wouldn't be the first time. His stepdad's a bully. Once he punched Kofi in the belly, pinned him to the floor with his knees and stuffed his mouth with raw mince till he was sick, and all because Kofi said he wanted to be a vegetarian.

Mac punches star-shaped holes in doors when he's fighting with Mum, but he's never hurt me.

"What's with the bag?" I ask.

"I'm going on holiday." He doesn't look like someone who is going on holiday—he's running from the dark not heading into the light. "Coming?"

I nod. "What do I need?"

"Me—that's all you need."

10

Kofi stole some white powder from the bully. His stepdad is short but solid, the kind of guy I'd hide behind if I was being chased, and this is the only way Kofi can hurt him back. We eat bananas and tiny kiddie boxes of sultanas, on our backs on a thin rolled-out mattress inside Kofi's tent and play our music thumping-loud to beat through the fog in our brains, holding hands like we're scared to be alone in the woods after dark. I pretend my other hand is holding Cee's.

"When I was younger, I thought I could live here," I say.

"Nah, nowhere to get your hair extensions done." Kofi laughs.

"We'd be alright for berries though." I laugh too, but he's right. Without hair appointments and visits to the Chinese nail bar or the studio to get my eyebrows threaded, my days would be spent at Tia's getting pissed and allowing quadrilateral equations or whatever they're called, and WW2 dates drummed into our heads in history lessons, to seep through the cracks in my brain and evaporate into the universe. I'm back in the film set of my life, the lonely, airbrushed victim wasting away in the woods until a bear pounces and gnaws on my bones.

"Shall we do it?" he says. His heart isn't in it though, I can tell even through the cyclone in my head.

"I used to have a bear-wolf." I declare this in past tense; I'm still not ready to share her with anyone else. I'm not sure I'll ever be ready, but without Cee there's too much space surrounding me, and nothing or no one else to fill it with.

Kofi props himself on one elbow and attempts to fix me with his wide brown eyes.

I laugh out loud. "Why you look at me like that, boy?"

"Tell me more," he says.

"She listened to me when I was sad. I used to have this thing where I would take my mum's jewellery if she left it on the side or hanging on the bathroom mirror, you know earrings, pendants, chokers, she was so careless, and she always had so much. So, I'd hide them under my bed until my mum or Gran took me to the park, sneak off when they weren't paying attention and stash it here with my bear-wolf."

"Very sneaky. Where is it now?"

"Probably still here somewhere." I picture my creature as I left her the day Kofi found me. "I brought a hairbrush and ribbons and everything and she used to let me style her." I sound like a five-year-old playing with Barbies or Bratz dolls. The Bratz mansion and convertible I had when I was five is still collecting dust in a cupboard in our spare room.

"Now that I'd like to see." Kofi's fingers stroke my hand. He sits up suddenly and my eyes take a second to adjust to his movement. "Let's go find her."

I wish I hadn't done the last line. It was more than a line, and my brain is humming and twitching, and I can't focus on what I need to say, can't get my story straight.

"I can't remember where she was now."

"Summer, it'll be like riding a bike, or having sex. You never forget. It's instinct, sweetheart." He's on his feet and dragging me upright.

"It's dark." Panic sets in. Not because I don't think I can find her but because I know I can. She's mine and I need to keep her safe for when she needs to keep me safe.

"Uh-huh."

"We'll get lost."

"I thought you was a big girl." He's still holding on to my hand like this is a thing now; we're doing this.

"I'm scared," I say. "We'll fall off a cliff and get impaled on a tree, or mutilated by wild cats, or, or we'll get raped by wolves."

"Whoa, you are one seriously fucked-up missy." Kofi pulls me close to his chest and strokes my hair and for once I don't care if it gets messed up, because he's warm, and my arms feel the way they feel in winter when you slip under the duvet and heat instantly smothers the cold, and you know you want to bury yourself in it from head to toe.

And as my nose is completely bunged up and crusty, I start crying big ugly sobs through my mouth, not only because I can't breathe, but because that's what I do when things are not going my way, and because I wish Kofi wasn't gay, and because I wish Cee was here.

"It's all my fault," I manage between sobs. "All my fault."

"Ritchie said we should put the tent up outside the square," Cee said. "Inside is haunted."

We were fourteen when we decided to spend the night in the

woods. I told Mum I was staying at Cee's cousin's house, and Cee told the Ovary she was with me. She never asked where.

The square was made up of stumpy wooden rafters, rotten and half-buried beneath weeds and moss and stringy roots like alien tentacles, so low you could step over them and miss them. It wasn't even complete. Ritchie told Cee it was once the foundations of a game-keeper's cottage. I had no idea how he knew this. It was easy enough to find with his directions; it was not so deep into the woods we'd get lost, and if we needed him, he'd know where to find us. Ritchie nearly always stayed out late at night and he made Cee promise we'd call him if we were scared, like in his head, that's exactly how he pictured the night going. And now there she was telling me the square was haunted.

At my wide eyes she laughed. "I'm joking. Chill." She'd untied a knot in the string holding the tent together and now fabric sheets were twisting and unfurling insanely around her legs.

"Do you know how to put up a tent?" I asked.

"Nope. Do you?" She stood on one section of polyester to hold it still. "Grab a pole."

By the time we finished threading poles and stamping on pegs, we had a shape that kind of resembled a tent for three-year-olds. The only way through the entrance flap was on hands and knees and there wasn't enough room inside for us to stretch out flat or stand up straight, but it was cosy, a surreal plastic home-for-two that made our faces look green and smelled like old wellies.

We were starving and thirsty. "Look what I brought." Cee raised her eyebrows and grinned as she rummaged around inside her rucksack. It was a small bottle of gin. She unscrewed the lid, took a noisy swig, and coughed as it went down. Then she handed the bottle to me. "Go on."

It burned all the way down and my cheeks felt like they were on fire. I screwed my eyes shut and waited for my head to cool down.

"I can't wait till I can go in pubs," Cee said. "I'll get pissed every night."

We sat outside on our backpacks, so our clothes didn't get damp in the night dew; it was steamy-hot inside, and condensation from our breath and the heat of our bodies formed on the inside of the tent and dripped onto our faces and arms. We ate the food Gran had packed for us, Jaffa cakes, ham sandwiches and strawberry laces, and saved the sausage rolls for breakfast. The gin we took turns at swigging straight from the bottle. There was no water to wash it down with and it went straight to our heads; we giggled at beetles with their fat black shells and their legs running at a hundred miles an hour; at the birds that chased each other around the treetops; at a squirrel who wanted our crumbs but was too scared to come close and take them.

"Go without then," Cee told it. "I love space," she said, laying back on the grass and staring beyond the treetops at the vast twilight above us. "There's nothing so beautiful in this world as stars. Look at them."

The vastness of the universe scared me, like who knew where it ended or what was out there or how far away it all was, and the gin was making the world slip away from me in lazy, spinning circles. I closed my eyes. I didn't need to look at the stars and the moon and the tree-arms that swayed because they were so high. I was content knowing my bear-wolf was close by. I was content knowing Cee.

"Do you want to know where I got the gin?" I sensed rather than saw her turn to face me in our patch of dark and turn back again to the stars. "Harry from the shop, you know, the one with the eyebrow piercing? He gave it to me for wanking him off."

Cee just dropped it into the dark of the forest like she'd shared a bar of chocolate with him, like she expected me to shrug and laugh it off. I couldn't. I couldn't even think about it and panic was setting in because I had no idea what to say. I breathed in deeply through my nose and filled my lungs with the smell of the woods, and gradually the trees settled into their spiralling shadow-shapes. I tried not to imagine they were skeletons.

"Have you kissed a boy?" Cee asked.

"No." My voice sounded lost in the darkness.

"I have. I kissed Harry and the Ovary's cousin. Well, he kissed me. He was working on some old banger in his garage and when he saw me, he said, 'Come in here, I got something to show you.' He got his cock out and rubbed it on my jeans. Made me put my hand on it." She paused like she was remembering how it felt. "It smelled of oil. His tongue was fat and slobbery, and after, I had to buy chewing gum to get rid of the feel of it."

Sometimes it felt like Cee was a million miles away from me, another planet away, and the nine months between us had somehow morphed into nine years. She always had stories to tell about boys. Boys always noticed Cee and, whatever it was they saw when they looked at her, it seemed they always gave her a story to tell. I wanted to catch up with her. I was scared she'd leave me behind, get with a guy who'd take her away from me, because I'd never find another friend to have adventures with like these.

I struggled to find something grown-up to say, so I blurted out, "I love space too."

"Summer?"

I'm on my back beside Kofi in the tent in the woods. My head feels like jelly, and I'm still bunged up, like one of those winter colds that lingers for weeks. I turn my head to glance at him and smile lazily.

"You talk in your sleep, has anyone ever told you that?"

"You're making it up." I stare at the tent roof. It feels like a sauna in here now and I watch condensation streak down the sides.

He props himself on one elbow and stares at me until I look at him. "Who gave Cee the pills?"

I blink, but I can't tear my eyes away from his enlarged pupils. I'm looking at Kofi, but seeing Cee, watching her head jerk forward, the shock in her eyes, the words dying on her lips. "She brought them with her," I whisper.

I can almost feel the relief in his shoulders. "Did she say where she got them?"

I shake my head. I would never have thought to ask.

"It's just . . . look . . . I know you feel responsible, Summer, but you didn't know she had a heart condition. You didn't force the pills down her throat." I close my eyes at the image in my head. "Maybe if you knew where she'd got them from, you might find a little closure."

I nod but I know I'll never find closure.

11

We lose time like grains of sand caught up in the tide. The only difference between dark and light is the opportunity to pee without worrying about splashing my jeans. I point out to Kofi, Cee's face etched on the moon. He tells me about his math teacher who's been doing things he shouldn't with a pupil. It isn't until we're physically starving, so hungry we start foraging on our hands and knees for berries and nuts and chasing squirrels to hunt down their stash of winter-food, that we decide to pack up and head back to town. The tent is smelly, underneath my nails are black, and Kofi is worried about his mum, but he needs to come back down to earth before he can head home.

We go straight to Tia's. She opens the door and says, "Fuck me, you stink. Where've you been?"

"Camping." We shrug like we don't care a rotten smell is hanging above our heads like a dirty brown cloud. We've only been gone two days. Three maybe. I think. "This is Kofi."

"Better not get too close," Kofi says, hovering behind me.

Frankie is in the living room. "You look a mess," she says.

"Cheers, I feel great." I flop onto the armchair with my legs swung over the arm rest, Kofi on the floor in front of me.

Tia's voice reaches us through the plasterboard wall, "Come and see Auntie Summer, Bliss."

Sam Smith is on the radio, but the air is silent, I realise, when Kofi leans his head back against my thigh, a barrier. I resist the urge to plunge my grubby fingers into his hair and then I spot the newspaper, the *Gazette* probably, open on the coffee table at a picture of a face I recognise. The Ovary. The headline reads: HEARTBROKEN MUM LAUNCHES DRUG AWARENESS CAMPAIGN.

Tia comes in with Bliss attached to her hip the way Cee used to carry Demi. Her waist is thickening already, and her jeans are undone. "Auntie Summer's back from the dead," she says. A look passes between her and Frankie.

"Hey, baby," I say. "Where's my snugs?" But Bliss is eyeing up Kofi, her dummy bobbing up and down, sleep-hair clinging to her cheeks. "That's it, forget your Auntie Summer now, Kofi is here."

I want to close my eyes. My phone's dead and I don't know what time it is, or even what day it is, but my eyes are stuck on the black and white image smiling at me from the pages on the coffee table.

"Thinks she's a fucking celebrity," Tia says following my gaze. She sets Bliss down on the floor with *The Hungry Caterpillar*. The book used to be mine. I wish I'd saved it for Jonah.

"She didn't even cry at the funeral," Frankie adds in.

"Clever though. She went with no makeup, so she looked proper rough," Tia says. "And she got slaughtered at the wake."

The words dangle from the ceiling like Halloween decorations. An image of the Ovary sprawled on a sofa, bottle of vodka on the floor and everyone giving her shoulders sympathy-pats, makes me want to puke. I should've been there. I'm sapped with the overwhelming belief that I was never there for Cee when she needed me.

"Bet she misses having a babysitter," Frankie says.

"They forget Summer was always there for Courtney." Tia shakes her head at Bliss who is about to pull the sparkly ribbon from her hair and launch it at Kofi. "Who did she share a bed with most nights? Who took her on that caravan holiday to Cromer? It wasn't that fat bitch, was it?"

"Where did she get the pills?" I blurt it out, the suggestion fresh in my mind from Kofi bringing up the subject in the tent. It has slithered its way inside my brain and nested there without me realising.

"You gave them to her," Tia frowns. "Didn't you?"

Kofi is rubbing my hands, and I'm hot and limp and shivering, but he lifts me up and says, "Guys, I think she needs some air." As he half carries me to the door, I hear him say, "FYI, no she didn't."

The house is empty when we get home. In the shower, I close my eyes and pretend I'm standing beneath a waterfall, in a rainforest with a perfect blue lagoon waiting for me on the other side, while in the kitchen Kofi cooks turkey dinosaurs and curly fries. On my bed, we eat in silence, our food smothered in tomato ketchup, empty plates wiped clean with bread and butter and, when Kofi has showered, we climb under the duvet and forget we're back.

There are dark shadows in the room when my bedroom door bursts open.

"What the fuck!" It's Mac.

Kofi is yanked off the bed, landing on his knees on the floor, his head banging off the bedside cabinet, and Mac is yelling at Mum, "Did you know about this?" He's dragging Kofi by his arm because he's only wearing boxers, and Kofi is reaching for his rucksack because all his stuff in the world is in there.

"I'm sorry,'" he mumbles. "I'm sorry. It was my fault."

"Too fucking right it's your fault." Mac is so loud. "What is wrong with you?"

Mum hovers in the doorway, hair all over the place, hands on hips, dark eyes taking it all in. "Shut up, Mac. Let him go."

I want to hug Kofi, wrap my arms around his head because no one ever hugs him close to their chest, but instead I stay in my bed, knees trembling and brain bouncing around inside my skull, waiting for the tears to come.

Mac shoves Kofi to the floor where he grabs his clothes and trainers and, clutching them tightly and says, "It's not what you think." He turns to my mum. "Miss Knight, you know I wouldn't do nothing wrong."

Mum shakes the thoughts from her head. "Just go. It's fine, just go."

"It is not fine." Mac's anger is a direct line to her, but Kofi is out the door, his footsteps bumping up the stairs. "She's fifteen years old for Christ's sake. Fifteen! She should be doing maths homework and watching bloody *Hollyoaks*. Christ." He swipes at his mouth with the back of his hand like his words are greasy. "Next thing you know she'll be fucking pregnant."

"Mac," Mum cuts through his rant. "It's fine."

"It's fine," he mimics her with a toss of his head. "Let's sweep it under the carpet, shall we? Your daughter doesn't come home for three days and when she does, she's shagging someone she dragged in with her, but we'll pretend it's fine, so Lizzie doesn't have to think about discipline."

She rolls her eyes, and I can feel the hard wire in her veins. "There's no harm done this time. She's spending time with her mates, and after what she's been through—"

"Yeah, yeah, let's all pussyfoot around and tell her we're proud of her. You're her mother. You're supposed to know where she is in the middle of the night. I knew I shouldn't have let it go." He's shaking, his chest expanding and contracting like he's run a marathon. "You give me all the old crap that I'm not her father and I can't tell her what to do, and now look."

"He's gay," she says simply.

"What?" Mac shakes imaginary raindrops from his head. "What?"

"He." She points up the stairs. "Is. Gay. So, all your fucking screaming was for nothing. He's gay. She's grieving. And I'm a shit mother."

The tears won't come. I'm dried out and crumpled like the dishcloth Gran hangs over the tap in the kitchen sink at night. I scrunch my eyes and scream, "Get out! Get out! GET OUT!"

They stop and stare at me. Mac drops his arms that were swinging like he was swatting flies.

Mum says, "Summer?" like she isn't sure it's me.

I bury my face in my pillow and make sobbing noises which turn into hysterical uncontrollable laughter, but within moments, I'm dragged backwards off the bed by strong hands, and thrust through the doorway.

"I'm not having it," Mac says, and I'm unsure if he's

speaking to me or Mum. "Get upstairs," this *is* aimed at me. "For once you're going to do something for us."

They go out and leave me with Jonah. Mac says Mum needs to get dressed up and get out of the house. The baby is asleep, and Mac lays out baby wipes, Sudocrem, and a couple of nappies by the Moses basket and tells me they'll be back in time for his next feed. *Bird Box* is on Netflix. I've been meaning to watch it but there's never a moment when the house, or the telly, or my mind, belongs to me. Wrapped in my dressing gown I settle on the sofa with a tub of chocolate ice cream and a spoon.

Sandra Bullock has been left with two kids and only one of them is hers. That's what happens. Cee said she never wanted kids when she grew up; she'd been stuck with Vinny, and Demi, and Drew (how old even was Drew?) and she'd have been stuck with the new baby too because the Ovary was selfish.

She went on holiday once, to Spain, and left the kids with Cee like she was the real parent; Gran said she was going to call social services because you don't have kids and then swan off with your mates on the piss, but if she did call them, they never came and checked. If you ask me, adults don't think these things through. They pop out babies like they never learned about contraception in school, and then complain when their lives are screwed.

The roof of my mouth is numb from the ice cream, but I spoon in another mouthful. Mac gets it, I think. Shagging Mum is important to him, but so is Jonah. More so. I've seen the way he strokes his tiny hands when he's feeding him, the way he bends down ever so slowly and plants a kiss on his forehead when he's on the changing mat, the way he wants the best for him. Sometimes I wish Mum would shut up and listen to him for once.

A scrawny pink fist waves at me from above the side of the Moses basket. There's no sound just a wave of a skinny arm, a corner of blue blanket. I check my phone but I can't remember what time they left; Mum was zipping up a new pair of thigh-length boots, and her nails were sparkly yellow which made my chipped acrylics look even more manky, and I wasn't paying attention, but I'm sure they didn't tell me to feed him.

At some point during the tub of ice cream, Jonah must wriggle out of his blanket because arms and legs, like puppets on sticks, appear in the air above the side of his bed. I cross the room and peek in. His face is flushed and damp, like he's squeezing out sobs, but the sound is still gentle, faint. I mute the telly. Bliss screamed when she was a baby: cold violent screams that pierce my brain still when I think about them. Demi used to wail relentlessly, a sound that was drawn out, pathetic, and deliberately selfish. I've heard Jonah cry before, I'm positive, but lack of sleep is somehow disguising the memory.

I sit back down. The tub is empty, my head is spinning, and cramps are raging through my abdomen. I close my eyes, and into my head pops something about a hospital appointment with the baby. What was it? Mac asked me to go, support my Mum, but I was grieving drunk after Cee and I might've fallen asleep, or stayed at Tia's or somewhere else. I can't even remember.

In the kitchen, I rummage through Mum's filing: a stack of ripped envelopes and crinkled coffee-stained papers in the corner of the counter. There's nothing. In the crap-drawer, I find tiny tubs of different coloured pills, Sellotape, drawing pins, globs of Blu-tac, batteries which are probably dead, string, two old mobile phones with cracked screens, and some out-of-date New Look vouchers. Down to their bedroom, driven now by the need to settle the argument in my head, I search under the bed through dusty suede boots, sweaty old trainers, *Harry Potter and the Prisoner of Azkaban*, Christmas decorations, all sorts of stuff; in the chest of drawers, I sort through knickers and boxers, eyelashes, a dildo, and some lubricating gel which she got from an Ann Summers party. Ugh!

Back to the living room and I remember the baby bag. Inside is a blue transparent plastic wallet filled with notes. I skim the bold titles. Find what I'm searching for—Jonah has Down's syndrome. That's what everyone was talking about when he was first born.

Something sparks in my head. A memory of us, me, Mum, and Cee, on the sofa with cans of lager, a horror film on the telly, and she told us, "This baby isn't going to be normal. I don't think I can handle it. Can you imagine me with a baby that isn't normal?"

Cee said, "There's no such thing as normal," and, "He's got his big sister to look out for him so that makes him a lucky little boy."

Or maybe I'm confusing the whole thing with an episode of *Eastenders*.

12

There are sirens and I'm dribbling. I roll on to my back, gritty-eyed and breathing through my mouth, crawling with panic. It's dark and when I sift through the ringing in my ears, I realise there are no sirens, only voices.

Mac shouting, "The kid's out of control, Liz." Bang. "She should've gone with your mum, let them deal with it." Slam. "When was the last time she went to school? What fucking chance has she got?"

"You make it sound like she'll end up in prison." Her voice is hoarse like she's been off her nut at a rave all night and I picture her yanking off her boots, mascara-streaked cheeks, and jeans already undone.

"Well, she isn't going to bloody finishing school in Switzerland."

A pause. I wonder if Jonah is in the room with them, cocooned in his bubble, oblivious to the world he's been born into.

"She fed him ice cream for fuck's sake!"

The tub was empty. I think. I close my eyes. *Think.*

Searching for Jonah's paperwork, I left the tub in the kitchen, the spoon resting on the lid. I'm sure I did. The light was on so I could read through the bills and bank statements and repeat prescriptions; I knocked the spoon on to the floor with my elbow and it clattered, and I thought it might wake him, but it didn't because he didn't cry out.

"I didn't feed him ice cream," I tell Cee.

She's sitting on the end of my bed in her *Friends* hoodie and jeans, on her phone, and she smiles at me, scrapes hair behind her ear.

They've gone quiet; they must've heard me speak.

"Shh." I hold a finger to my lips and Cee nods.

She used to feed her babies ice cream. That's what she called them, her babies, Demi's favourite was strawberry; straw-bee she said because she couldn't pronounce it correctly.

"You just sleep while I clean him up!" Mac yells from upstairs, louder now. He's yelling at me. Then he murmurs gentle words to the baby, an apology probably.

"Oh, that's it, Mac the martyr!" Mum shouts. "So much better than us. Why don't you leave my daughter alone?"

I roll my eyes at Cee, but she doesn't appear to notice; she's chewing her bottom lip the way she always did when she was waiting for a boy to message her.

"Your daughter? She's yours until you want me to buy her something. Get her up. She can clear up the fucking mess she's made."

"He's your son. You clear up the fucking mess. You wanted him!"

I hold my breath, cement my bedroom door to its frame so they can't burst in.

"I don't think I can handle it," she said to us. "The baby won't be normal."

Jonah's not normal. I'm not normal. She only thinks she's normal.

"No one ever got anywhere being normal," Cee whispers from the end of the bed.

The boys treated us like princesses.

Last summer we paraded along the seafront like a production crew in our oversized sunglasses and our big-brand trainers. Pedestrians moved out of our way, stared at us. Cars honked and yelled out unintelligible words and children admired us, wanted to be one of us. We were beautiful.

Boots removed, the sea bit our ankles and we splashed each other, growing heavier and bolder until we flopped on to the beach, drenched, salty. We lay there until the sun hid behind a forest of clouds and the chill turned our pale skin to bobbles. Then we ate piping hot chips from paper, drank beer from icy bottles that the lads fetched outside from the bar, and one of them snuggled his leather jacket across my shoulders to keep me warm. The jacket smelt of digestives and dogs, but the beer had made my head fuzzy, and I nuzzled it without thinking. His hand was still on the jacket and I nuzzled his hand too, but I didn't care. I was a princess.

I felt out of sorts with Cee all wild and weird. Grandad used to keep tropical fish when the conversation focused mostly on his fake bad back and print smudges from the newspaper on the armchair, and when the fish became sick and dying, they buckled and jerked in their desperate attempts to breathe and stay alive. Cee reminded me of them sometimes: cold vacant eyes and desperation.

We played on the slot machines, changed pound coins into two pence pieces, pushed them into the slots and watched, hypnotised, as the shovels slid back and forth, back and forth, waiting for our winnings. We spread out. Jacket-man stuck with me. I felt his breath on my neck, beer and cigarette breath. I won a tacky plastic keyring, and he cheered, threw his arms up so everyone knew I'd won. I smiled up at him.

Tinny tunes jangled for attention and flashing lights popped up all around with dollar signs, and ker-pows, and treble-your-chances. Cheeks glistened. Eyes concentrated on the jackpot.

Ritchie's skinny new girlfriend with her nose piercing and her transparent T-shirt, draped his shoulder with her long blonde hair and licked his ear while he pumped coins into the fruit machines. He was oblivious to the leather jacket warming my shoulders despite the fact my eyes followed him everywhere.

We congregated around the baby rides at the front of the arcade: the shiny metal horses pulling an unstable wagon; the rusty red fire engine; the rainbow-coloured hot air balloon that rotated like a mini big wheel.

"Dare you to go on it," said jacket-man. He offered me a pound coin.

I hesitated. A woman with a little girl bundled up in a pink duffel-coat and shiny red boots, gave me snake-eyes and dragged her daughter away by the hand. The child craned her neck, looked behind her, not at the ride, but at me. Cee was laughing with some guy wearing a North Face cap.

I grabbed her hand and said, "Come with me."

Her eyes took in the plastic bucket-seat, the rainbow, the excitement in my eyes. "We'll break it," she said.

"Please." She saw the jacket around my shoulders, and

everyone waiting, and nodded. I wasn't strong like she was. I couldn't do it alone.

I climbed on first. It was uncomfortable, the seat bit into my hips, my feet touched the floor and my knees inched toward my chest until Cee sat on my lap and flattened them.

Everyone laughed. Ritchie and T-shirt girl had joined the rest of the gang, hugging each other's pockets. Jacket-man inserted the coin and the wheel creaked into motion taking us, legs out at ninety degrees and my arms around Cee's waist so she didn't slide off, upwards above their heads. The juddering snail-pace made me feel queasy like in Grandad's car, but I grinned into the crowd anyway. This was how it felt to be special, not Baby-girl special when I kicked off because I didn't want to go to school, but admired, adored, wanted. I imagined that moment bottled, smelling of concert-crowds and lip balm, and labelled 'Special' in a fancy curly font.

Cee slid off my lap before the ride stopped, and I followed to claps and cheers and laughter, but either the attendant had seen us, or someone had told him we were abusing the kiddie rides.

"Get out!" he shouted from behind Ritchie and his girl. "Get out, the lot of you." He was red in the face and his belly bulging above the belt holding up his jeans.

We piled outside, everyone laughing and jostling, and rubbing my shoulder, saying, "Good girl," and, "Brilliant," and, "Classic."

Cee and I linked arms. I knew she felt special too when we were together.

13

Ritchie is everywhere.

I can't remember where he's been when he was away, but he's thinner, darker, sadder, and my heart rips open all over again. Hong Kong, Singapore maybe, somewhere hot and steamy, and overpopulated, where he could get lost in a crowd, earn some decent money and airlift Cee away from here.

"I don't even care if the plane crashes with me on it," she said. "At least I'll die knowing I was leaving."

Leaving me behind would've made her miserable, I know, but from the moment she told me she might go away, I lived our adventures with the pain of having already lost her. When she giggled at my morning bed-hair I told her to piss off, knowing that one day she would; when we got drunk at Tia's and top-and-tailed on the sofa, I dreaded the day I'd have the furniture to myself.

He lights a fag at the end of the street, head down, hands cupped around his face, and his shoulders are the shoulders of someone who isn't supposed to be here in this place, with the shadow of his lost sister clinging to his neck. He doesn't notice me. He folds himself around Michaela from the hair salon even though she's shagging one of the bouncers from the Venue, and she told Tia her ex-boyfriend gave her chlamydia.

The next day he's leaving the bakers with a sausage roll in a white paper bag as I'm heading towards the Chinese studio to get my brows threaded. I raise an arm and wave at him. What Kofi said in the tent has been playing on my mind and I want to ask Ritchie if he knows where Cee got the pills from, but he takes one look at me, and the expression on his face is so filled with hate, I almost don't recognise him before he walks away.

He used to look out for us. When everyone was at the park, he waited outside the crumbling toilets while Cee changed her clothes, made sure we got home if we were mad-drunk, gave us the dry patches of grass to sit on; it was an opening-doors kind of thing. Respect. But now, he wouldn't even notice me if I were about to step in front of the traffic and that breaks my heart all over again. What's left of it.

The next weekend, I'm out with Tia and Frankie because Danielle and her boyfriend are getting a takeaway with Mum and Mac, and I can't face sitting in my room listening to them. We're on our third round of cocktails when Ritchie walks into the Hole in the Wall with some guys I don't recognise. I sip my Porn Star, half-listen to the conversation about a new clinic in town doing lip infills for a hundred-and-fifty quid special offer for the next month and watch Ritchie from behind my straw. His gaze sweeps the room, but I lean behind Frankie and ask her if she wants to do karaoke. I hate karaoke. When she says yes, I wish my brain, in panic mode, could've conjured up something more imaginative.

She drags me up to the DJ, tells him we'll do 'Dancing Queen' and locks her arm with mine so there's no escape.

"This is for you, Tia." She breathes into the microphone and pointing in the general direction of our table, which I can't see because there's a light directly behind Tia which is making the others look like they're in some weird kind of kaleidoscope.

We are awful. After three drinks and half a bottle of peach schnapps, I can't even remember the words to an Abba song that everyone in the entire world knows the words to. Everyone is laughing at us, and the more they laugh, the more holes appear in my song lyric repertoire.

Tia stands and howls, "Whoop-whoop." Everyone is singing along. And I watch Ritchie's expression alter in slow motion, as he recognises me, takes in the gold shorts and stilettos, and chucks a twenty onto the bar before he leaves.

The beauty salon is a shed in the woman's back garden which has a real swimming pool sunk into the ground, with palm trees in terracotta pots, and a brick barbecue as big as our kitchen. There are four of us: me, Tia, Frankie, and the groom's niece Bella who is eleven. We pile inside, embarrassing the silence with our excitement, and our busyness, and the clunk of our bags on the tiled floor. I'm as loud as the rest of them; it's the only way to pretend there isn't a giant ravine into which the fifth person has slipped, and because if I shut up and acknowledge that she isn't here, that her arm isn't linked with mine, I'll slide into the same ravine, falling until my head hits the ground and splits like an egg.

The decor is pale grey and silver, a bed in the middle of the room draped with fluffy grey towels and blankets, silver flowers in a vase in the window and a sparkly painting of silver trees against a winter sky on the wall. The air inside is so pristine and pretty, I'm certain I can smell last night's McDonald's on my breath.

"Find a seat," Crystal says in her lavender-scented voice. She flicks through the pages of a neat silver backed diary as a tiny terrier snoops in sniffing at our ankles. Bella is on the floor stroking the dog as Crystal glances up to take our names. The fake smile and fake tan fade. "What's she doing here?" she says with a nod in my direction.

"Summer? She's bridesmaid." Tia winks at me like this is a game of *Guess Who?*

But the silver has lost its sparkle; the silence is swollen with gentle music which, instead of relaxing my shoulders, is scrubbing away at my nerve ends; even the dog is nipping at Bella's fingertips building up to claiming a chunk of flesh.

Crystal shakes her head, mouth turned down. "I'm not doing her makeup."

"What the hell?" I say. They're all staring at me. Silent. Choosing sides because they want their makeup done for nothing. I stand, snatch at my bag straps, and hoist it onto my shoulder, wobbly in my heels.

No one else stands. No one follows me to the door or stops the annoying little fucker from nipping at my ankles.

"I'll sort something out, Sum," Tia finally says, suddenly fascinated by her toenails which, I think, have never suited her painted nude. She has fat toes. "It'll be alright."

Sure it will, I think.

In the back room of her boutique, Gran slips me a hundred quid and squeezes my hand. "Stay strong, girl," she says. "You're better than that lot. Look at you. You've got more love in your little finger than they've got between them. And you're beautiful."

I switch off after that. It's like they eat these words for dinner and regurgitate them whenever they're confronted with a difficult situation.

"Stayed out all night? Good girl, staying safe."

"Didn't go to school last month? She'll learn more from life experience than geography class."

"Involved in a drug-driving accident? Stay strong, baby girl. We're so proud of you."

On my way out, I slip a pair of diamante studs from a clear plastic rack above the belts and into my pocket. Jamal, colour coordinating the chiffon rail, is too scared to say anything since the time I sucked him off in the stock room while Gran was chatting to some old dear with pink baby-doll hair. He's gay anyways.

I chuck the earrings before I get home. I've been remembering, as clear as if it were yesterday, the first time I discovered my bear-wolf. I thought she was a real-live bear when I was four, a real-live bear who'd eat anyone who came near her apart from me, because she loved me.

"Jack and Jill went up the hill." I remember singing to the patches of blue between the twig-arms and the leaf-hats the trees wore, my arms stretched around my yellow ball that smelled of rubber and stuck to my skin.

Ahead of me, Mummy held hands with her current boyfriend, new-Billy, because first Billy was just Billy. Her ponytail swung from side to side and their hands, joined, swung back and forth. Occasionally they glanced into each other's eyes. They didn't look behind them. They didn't hear me sing.

When we reached the park, new-Billy bounced me up and down on the seesaw and pushed me on the big swings with my hair blown stringy, and I forgot the nursery rhyme and sang one of Mummy's songs that she danced around the dining table to with a cigarette in her hand.

Mummy smiled with squashed lips. "Early night, tonight," she said, because I wore Mummy out.

I dropped my ball and it rolled into the nasty prickly bushes. We took the shortcut through the woods to the park, but in the summer the bushes spread wild and spiteful around the trees, and sticky stuff was everywhere, clinging to socks and trainers and legs if you weren't careful. Sometimes I wasn't careful and got all rashy, and Gran painted me white and gave me chocolate ice cream.

I didn't know where the woods came from, but they were there, backed on to our estate on one side and reaching to Timbuktu on the other, and if you followed the path, you came out at the park. They built a wooden castle in the playground after the winter. I wasn't allowed to climb inside it in case I scuffed my shoes, or my knees.

I squinted inside the bush, but I couldn't see my ball. Mummy and new-Billy were still walking, almost at the top of the hill where the woods stopped, and the park began. I couldn't hear what they were saying but I could just make out the black mark on the back of Mummy's jeans that she didn't know was there. If the black mark vanished, I thought, I wouldn't get my ball back and that kind of scared me.

I held my breath. Wooden fingers cracked beneath my feet as I left the path. Snuggled inside the bush was a hollow like a cave and watching me from inside the hollow, were shiny golden eyes. I felt a low rumble in my chest like when a cat purrs because it wants you to believe it is nice.

I glanced at Mummy and new-Billy still walking, still in love, and back to my ball which was just sitting there. One more glance in Mummy's direction before I dropped to my knees on the raggedy nettle carpet. My knees stung but I ignored the pain and crawled closer to the bush, and closer to the eyes. I reached out with one hand.

"Summer!" There were knots in her voice.

I pushed my face through the gap in the bush, the way I did at home in the bath, pushing my face through the surface of the water when I wanted to make my doll's hair go wavy, and blinked. The dark turned fuzzy. I opened my eyes wider until the cave-eyes grew a black furry face and a mouth with sharp teeth. A bear.

"SUMMER!"

I turned my head, startled to hear my name, and in that moment, my ball rolled back to me, knocked against my knees, stopped right there.

Mummy's strides were wide and strong, not slow and frail the way they were when she walked beside new-Billy, her face filled with clouds. She grabbed at my shoulder to drag me upright as I clutched my ball.

"Look at the state of your jeans. Ruined," she complained, shaking my shoulders. Her face was pink, her eyes small. I held on tight to my ball and my teeth.

"It's only a bit of dirt," said new-Billy from behind her. "It'll brush off when it's dry." Mummy's eyes filled with tears; her hands helpless. "Come on, don't let it spoil our day. It's only a pair of jeans." He took her hands, smiled into her eyes, and she melted.

They joined hips as they walked away. "Stay with us," new-Billy called over their shoulders.

I lingered, caught between my bear and Mummy, until new-Billy snapped, "Summer!" and then I walked sideways like a crab, clinging to the bear's hollow with my sticky eyes so I wouldn't forget.

I wish Cee had known my bear-wolf.

14

Once, we had a problem with our Freeview box, before Grandad paid for us to get Sky, like a loose connection—the programmes were there but they would crackle with static and the frames would freeze, so Sienna would be silent-angry for a full minute on *Hollyoaks,* and Sharon would be staring, mid-cup of tea on *Eastenders,* while the box sorted itself out.

Mum is the same. There's a loose connection somewhere. She rides her exercise bike until she melts into a puddle of sweat on the carpet. She paints her nails, plucks her eyebrows, smokes on the balcony, plays Candy Crush, watches Netflix, all of these things natural like a polar bear rolling in snow; but when she feeds Jonah, she doesn't hold him close, doesn't rock him to sleep, doesn't whisper gentle words while she's winding him, or stroke his hair when he's asleep. There's a loose connection. The movements are there but the ends are frayed and picking apart at the seams so the stuffing spills out.

She always talks too much, talks over people and doesn't come up for air. Now she lets the phone ring even when she knows it'll be Gran.

"Leave it," she snarls from behind a trail of nicotine. And she rolls her eyes when I pick up.

"Hi, Gran." I smile into the phone.

"Tell her I'm busy," she mouths.

"Oh, she's here, Gran," I say. "She doesn't want to speak to you."

The phone sags with the weight of her shoulders, and Mum gives me evils, but I don't regret saying what I said. It's true.

Gran puffs air into the phone. "What happened about the wedding makeup?" she asks. "Did Tia get it sorted?"

"No," I say.

"So, she didn't even back you up, put in a good word, like?"

"No." I don't want to think about it. Her fiancé's family are paying for the makeup and the hair, and pretty much everything else, and if she rocks the boat, Tia will have to fork out for it herself. The money's more important to her.

"Well don't worry, you'll still be the most gorgeous bridesmaid. I never did like her. Just like her bloody mother."

They always say that.

Mum waits until her stomach is flat before she goes out again. You can smell the perfume from outside. The walls vibrate along to the music, and she's three quarters through a bottle of Pinot before the hotpants are zipped up and the heels are buckled.

"What?" she speaks to me through the mirror.

"Where are you going?"

"Out with Dan. It's doing my head in; I need to get out." Mum turns her head from side to side, pouts and smooths on red lipstick, gold earrings flapping against her cheeks.

"What about Jonah?"

She packs lipstick, perfume, and eye liner into a small glitzy clutch bag. Her gaze darts about the room until she locates her leather handbag beside the bedside cabinet.

"Pass me my purse, babe." It's too bulky to fit in the clutch bag so she removes some notes and coins and slips them in loose. When she stands, she's about twelve inches taller than me. "There's a bottle made up in the fridge. He can have it when he wakes up."

She waits for me to tell her she looks lovely, a princess, so I deliberately say nothing.

"Mac won't be late. He'll know what to do." She bends, studies her reflection one last time, tugs at the curls swimming around her forehead.

"I know what to do," I say.

Mac brings home fish and chips, and we don't even bother putting the food on plates but eat out of thick white paper, the smell of vinegar obliterating the lingering clouds of Dior J'adore. He showers while I give Jonah his bottle. More bottles are made up. Mac says, "Shit," each time he loses count of the spoons full of powdered milk. His hair is wet, and a tea towel is slung over his shoulder when he pokes his head through the doorway and says, "Stick a film on then, Summer. Just got to pop out quickly."

While he's out, I choose *Isn't it Romantic* with Rebel Wilson, even though I know Mac won't enjoy it. I need something easy: a film I don't need to concentrate on.

We sit on the sofa with Jonah between us smelling of Johnson's baby powder and milk burps. He's not snuggled in a blanket and his limbs enjoy the freedom, legs folding in on themselves and arms waving about throwing tiny feeble punches against my arm. My hair falls onto his face when I bend over him and he scrunches his eyes closed and blinks furiously, his head twisting from side to side on his fragile neck to escape the tickles.

Mac swigs from a bottle of beer and laughs. "He likes that."

"Did you like that, baby?" I say offering him a finger which he clings to like it might just save his life. His fingers are so narrow, his fingernails so tiny they make me think of sparrows, or robins, weightless breakable birds to be scooped up and swaddled in cosy lined nests to keep them safe.

We barely watch the movie. We stare at Jonah as if we're in an episode of *Doctor Who*: blink and he'll vanish. There's no gossip, no bowls of cereal substituted for dinner, no phone calls to Danielle that drag on for hours, the phone carried out to the balcony along with a packet of cigarettes and a can of Coke.

Mac strokes the baby's arm. "What's this shite you're watching, Summer? There must've been a Marvel film or something we could've watched."

"It's good," I say. "And you did tell me to choose."

"I'm joking," he says. "It's good to see a bit of colour in your cheeks, but when my boy's older he's not watching no rom-coms, okay?"

"Okay."

"I can't wait to take him to his first football match."

"I can't wait to paint his nails."

"You've got *no* chance."

"You try and stop me."

Despite the baby's presence between us on the sofa, it feels like the first time we've ever been alone. Before, when Mum went on a night out, Mac stayed out too, or I went to the park with Cee, or we took a bottle of vodka down to my room and listened to music or watched a horror on the iPad. Mac's okay when he isn't trying to be my dad. I even catch him smiling at the telly when he thinks I'm not paying attention.

My phone pings. It's a message from Tia.

Jay invited Ritchie to the wedding, soz babe. X

"What's wrong?" Mac asks.

I shake my head. "Nothing."

"The face doesn't look like it's nothing," Mac says. He reaches for my hand and waits for me to look at him. "Come on, you can talk to me."

The baby swings an arm my way and I catch it and kiss the back of his hand. I wish I was a baby again, with no memories, no knowledge, no missed turnings, or impossible future. It would be bliss having nothing to do but eat, sleep and play. Like a whiteboard fresh out of the box, no mistakes, no irreversible shadows.

"Is it about Courtney?" Mac asks.

"No." I bury my face against Jonah's soft belly.

"Are you telling porkie-pies?" Mac laughs.

"I'm not five," I say, but I smile anyways.

"What is it then?"

"It's the wedding." I can't tell him what happened at the beauty salon; it's embarrassing, and he'll think I'm a right loser, and more importantly I don't want him to side with them. "Cee's brother is invited."

He strokes the baby's cheek with the back of a finger, rests his head against the back of the sofa. "Is that a problem?"

Don't cry. Don't cry. Don't cry, I tell myself.

The expression on Ritchie's face when he chucked his money on the bar is all I need to know about how this will go, there'll be pointing and whispering, an elbow in the back, drinks spilt until I accept defeat and leave. If Ritchie is there, others will be there too. I won't stand a chance.

"I can't even get my bridesmaid makeup done."

"Summer, look." He reaches for my hand and squeezes it. "Courtney was your friend, and, whatever the circumstances, you're grieving, the same way her family are grieving. Don't put yourself in situations where you'll only be made to feel worse. You're vulnerable. You need to surround yourself with people who won't drag you down. People who have your interests at heart."

"What do you mean?" My voice has somehow regressed back to my five-year-old voice, and I cough to clear my throat.

"Well, how important is this wedding to you? And don't look at me like that," he says as I pull my hand away. "I know you're a bridesmaid, but how important is it that you stay for the party? Tia forgets you're only fifteen. Everyone does."

He doesn't make it sound like this is a good thing, and I feel the way I felt in primary school, when I tried to crawl into the playhouse and some girls blocked the entrance with their legs spread and their arms crossed and their evil snake-stares. It was Kofi who made them move aside and let me in, but I felt so small and insignificant, that I went to the sandpit instead. And after school I screamed until Mum took me to the Cross Crab where they had the kids' soft play area. I ate sweets, and waited at the bottom of the big slide, and threw balls at the other kids.

"It's only a party, Summer. There'll be plenty more parties."
He shrugs.

I message Tia.

I can't stay if he's there.

One eye on the phone, I tickle the soles of Jonah's feet until
her reply comes back.

*You still coming to the hen do? We'll be short on numbers if you're
not coming.*

15

Mum gets a taste for going out the way most people get a taste for caffeine or chocolate. With her legs uncovered and a mini avalanche of chains around her neck, she creates a cloud of noise around her getting-ready sessions that plummets the house into a weird kind of library-silence when the door closes behind her. When she's gone, we breathe.

I spread a blanket on the living room floor and play with Jonah, which mostly means letting him kick my chest as I lean over him or letting him grab handfuls of hair and tug until my scalp tingles; for a baby he's got some muscles. He doesn't smile yet, but I think he enjoys it.

I give him a bottle and wait for Mac to come home with food; because Mum survives on cereal and large white tablets, it doesn't occur to her that the rest of mankind might require a diet with a bit more variety. Even Danielle when she visits, has evolved into a slippery eel from which her two toddlers slip and slide as if she's covered in oil. Maybe she's covered in oil. I imagine them, her and Mum, slithering in and out of clubs, the bouncers' heads spinning, as they ask each other, "Did you see that?"

Gran leaves Jamal to close the shop so she can visit us

early before Mum goes out. She chats to Mum through the bedroom doorway, her wine-conversation competing with the music which bounces off the ceiling.

When she stays home, I climb into my bed and stare at the ceiling, watching imaginary spiders racing back and forth and spinning webs that I'm scared will one day fall on to my face while I sleep and suffocate me. I wonder if my lips will turn blue.

Cee says they probably will. "I think that's just what happens. It won't hurt though, promise."

Sometimes she stretches out beside me on the bed, and we both follow the spiders, fingers touching beneath the duvet.

"Tell me what's been going on," she whispers.

I tell her the good bits about Jonah, Mac, and Kofi. When I think about everything else, I'm like a wasp trapped inside a pint glass, buzzing for a way out and banging my head against the glass wall until I give up. Tom hasn't contacted me since the accident. No boys message me now.

I missed it at first—the attention. I felt the way I felt when my dad, my real dad, visited and promised to call on Sundays. He knelt on the kitchen floor in front of me.

"I've told Lizzie I'll call you every Sunday, Summer. Okay?" He'd watched Mum's face, waiting for a gold star or a big tick. "Promise. So, when it's Sunday and you hear the phone ring, you pick it up like a good girl." He held my arms and kissed my forehead. "And no more of this sneaking around the house crap. You'll scare the living daylights out of someone one of these days." Then he was gone.

Every morning I asked, "Is it Sunday?"

"Jesus, Summer!" Mum said on the third day. "You don't go to school on bloody Sundays."

On the day Mum said it was Sunday, I watched the phone all day. Gran came around and asked Mum what I was doing, and she said, "Waiting for that fucking useless piece of shit to prove he isn't a liar."

And Gran nodded her head.

My dad didn't call on Sunday. He didn't call for six weeks and when the phone did ring, it was Saturday and Mum answered. "Funny fucking Sunday this," she said.

But I'd already forgotten how to see his face when I closed my eyes.

The evenings when it's me, Mac, and Jonah, we settle into a pattern of watching telly and snuggling on the sofa with Jonah between us like our umbilical cord. The movies are deliberately forgettable, even the superhero ones chosen by Mac, and I soon forget to tense my shoulders waiting for him to mention school, and he forgets to accuse me of being lazy when he fetches us both a drink from the fridge.

"I've done some research," he says halfway through *The Princess Diaries*. "When he's older we can experiment with his diet. Certain foods can help with development, and with behavioural problems, like the two of them can go hand in hand."

"What kind of food, like vegetables?"

"Well not only vegetables but cutting out dairy or gluten might help. I need to look into it more, but my mum will get us registered with a group of parents all dealing with the same syndrome. It'll be good to meet up with other people, you know. If they've tried stuff and it worked then it'll save us time."

He doesn't elaborate, and I don't ask. My brain isn't capable of processing all this medical stuff.

For a while we watch Jonah, his tongue still too large for his mouth, his eyes focused on the starry lights still fixed around the window frame since last Christmas. She'll never agree to the group thing especially if Mac's mum has any involvement. It'll send her into a tailspin, and I know exactly what she'll say. "I'll sort out my own child, thank you very much. I don't need any hippy group therapy sessions where everyone chants and channels the universe into making their kids normal."

"Your mum's all for it," he says as if reading my thoughts.

She must not have been sober when she agreed.

"And we can all learn sign language."

It's the first time anyone has spoken about Jonah's hearing. He has thickener added to his bottles because he has reflux and without it, the milk comes straight back out, but now, with the words spoken aloud about his hearing, it all starts to make sense: the way Mac communicates with the baby through touch rather than words, Mum's untamed music, and her inability to communicate, when talking is literally her life.

An image flashes into my head of Mac and Jonah at a football match, Jonah wearing a bobble hat and vacant stare, while around him everyone cheers their team's winning goal, and Mac on his knees signing the score to him. Tears sting my eyes.

Mac's fingers form shapes in front of me.

"What's that?" I ask.

"Jonah." His grin is filled with pride.

"You made that up," I say.

"I saw it on YouTube so it must be right."

Heads together, we pass the evening watching videos and practising signing all our names. Mac shares a beer with me—we both know I'm not going to school any time soon—and we giggle because I'm left-handed, and the letters of the alphabet look completely wrong when I sign them.

"Cack-handed," Mac says.

"That's something Gran would say."

We're laughing at my cack-hands when Mum walks in earlier than usual, eyebrows intact, hair dry, and eyes still able to focus when spoken to.

"What's so funny?" she asks. Her voice says that whatever it is, the joke didn't quite reach her. Her mood reacts with ours like a chemistry experiment. I realise how comfortable I've been with Mac and Jonah, easy the way it was with Cee, and now everything feels wrong again, like the room has turned blue, and it hits me like a punch in the gut how much I miss her. Maybe it will always be this way.

"Did you know your daughter has cack-hands?" Mac is barely upright on the sofa, one leg sprawled across the arm, bare foot swinging frighteningly close to Mum's thigh.

She doesn't smile. Her gaze takes in my open dressing gown and Minnie Mouse pyjamas, Mac's fingers near my shoulder, and the baby as an afterthought.

"What's that supposed to mean?" she asks, eye narrowed like he's speaking another language.

"We've been learning how to sign our names and she's rubbish." He's still laughing, deliberately reaching his toes towards her, knowing how she feels about feet.

"I'm better than you," I say.

Mac sits forward, reaches for her hand but she bats his arm away.

"Don't touch me," she says.

"Wait, what have I done?" His gaze flickers between the two of us. "What's happened?"

"You tell me." Her eyes are like slits despite the curve of eye liner. "I don't expect to come home and find the two of you playing silly buggers." Her chest is heaving like she ran all the way from town.

"Oh okay, so you call staying home with our son, 'playing silly buggers'? So, what, you'd rather we sat here in silence waiting for you to remember we exist?" His hand is on the baby's legs, protective.

"Summer, go to your room," she says without looking at me.

"Bit late for that." Mac gathers Jonah carefully into his arms and wraps a soft grey blanket around him.

"What, Mac? Say what you mean."

I wish she'd stand aside so I could slip between them unnoticed and go to my room. There's cold metal in the air with her arrival. I want to snatch Jonah, smother him in bubble-wrap and post him to somewhere far away, where mothers have tits that touch their belly buttons, and floral aprons tied around their waists while they bake buttery shortbread. But Mac is holding him close to his chest.

"You, doing the whole discipline thing now," he says.

"Fuck off." She whirls on her heels and marches into the kitchen where cupboard doors slam, and cutlery is thrown across the counter. The mugs topple from the mug-tree.

"Very mature!" Mac yells. "Let's set an example, eh?"

"I'm obviously not good enough for that," she yells back.

"Maybe if you stayed in, you'd learn."

Mac follows her, and I grab the opportunity to run downstairs and hide in my bedroom. I pull the duvet over my head, look at Cee's Instagram where all the pictures of me and her have been deleted, and wait for them to stop.

For the next week she stays in, proving to herself, to us, that she can do it, she can be in the house without feeling trapped. I watch her. When I was little, I threw my Bratz convertible across the room once, snapping the driver door from its hinges and smashing to smithereens a limited-edition Cinderella figurine Gran had bought when I was born, and all because I wanted pizza for breakfast. She made me pizza for breakfast, and I ate half a slice and said I felt sick. The following day I ate coco pops, and Gran replaced Cinderella with a less limited and more plastic replica.

There's a hatch between our kitchen and the dead end of the living room. Sometimes Gran sits at the four-seat table by the hatch, flicking through a glossy magazine so their conversations don't have to breathe when Mum pops to the kitchen for a beer or a can of Coke. It feels like she wrapped Jonah up in a bundle and posted him through the hatch for someone else to catch the other side.

Mum cooks meals: spaghetti Bolognese, sausages and mash, chicken korma from a jar. She makes up bottles of baby milk, vacuums the living room carpet, cleans the bath, and she tiptoes around us as though we're not to be woken or she'll die a long and painful death.

When she's on the bike, I deliberately take Jonah out of the

Moses basket and change his nappy, even if it doesn't need changing. I stroke his face with my hair and giggle when he squirms. I pray for him to smile at me.

Mum wipes her face with a towel, lights a cigarette, stands on the balcony with her bony arse facing us, picking at her lips while she waits for a magical creature to emerge from the woods and excite her.

While I feed him, Mum starts dinner preparations, or tidies the cupboard under the sink, or shaves her legs. She helps Gran in the shop on Jamal's day off and comes home with a carrier bag stuffed with ripped jeans, silver belts, and an off-the-shoulder glitter top. Silver is the new gold.

"When are you seeing Tia?" she asks.

"I don't know." I shrug.

"You look like a ghost, Summer. You need to get out there instead of wasting your life in that bloody dressing gown. Put some makeup on. Make yourself look pretty."

Because pretty is perfect.

16

"You miss her, don't you?" Mac asks me.

Mum has gone to the cinema with Danielle to watch *Rocket Man*. They're not drinking; she won't be late and I'm counting the minutes, dreading the halfway point at which there'll be less time ahead of us than behind us until she comes home. It's the noise, I tell myself, the way she takes over, fills the space, and owns our thoughts. But this isn't true.

"Yeah," my voice is soggy with tears.

Apart from Mum barking her well-rehearsed lines, "Get out there and show them you're strong," and, "You were her best friend, don't let them forget it," no one mentions Cee.

Mum says these things for her benefit, not mine. She's 'doing her bit' showing some compassion, reminding herself that she was practically Cee's mum because God knows her own mother never did anything for her. Gran pussyfoots around me. Like I can see in her eyes she thinks I should be going out, seeing my mates, getting drunk and doing teenager stuff, and then she remembers what happened and she swallows her thoughts, drowns them with another cuppa, flicks through another magazine.

But without Cee's light I don't know where to go. Without

her watching my back I feel the stab wounds every single day and I don't know how to heal them. I've tried reliving that night, but I can't get beyond Cee's blue lips and empty eyes. And always, overshadowing everything else, there's me being needy on the phone with her.

"Look, I'm not going to pretend I know how you feel," Mac says. "I'm not going to say forget all about it and move on. But I will say this: you can't sit around for the rest of your life wishing things were different. You want things to be different, do something about it. The world won't come to you."

I nod and bend to kiss the tip of Jonah's nose, so he doesn't see my watery eyes, the tears that grow so big and then recede like the tide on its way back out. My throat aches with the weight of them.

"It's so hard though," I say, straightening.

"Uh-huh. Anyone who tells you it's easy is lying. And you know what, youngsters make things worse for themselves, living their best lives on bloody social media. Get out there. Do something real. See the world. Meet people."

It's easy for him to say. He has a job, a baby, my mum. He can do whatever he wants, whenever he wants, and his path is drawn on a map with arrows pointing the way.

"And you'd do yourself a favour if you stop hanging around with knob-heads."

I smile. "All boys are knob-heads."

"I didn't mean the boys." He studies the telly. "Seriously though, you need to set yourself some standards, girl. Draw some lines."

"But boys don't want girlfriends these days. They just want a shag." My cheeks grow hot when I say the word like I've never said it before, like I've not known this since I was thirteen, like I should still be playing with dolls.

"You're forgetting one very important thing, Summer. You're underage. They're committing a crime. End of. You don't even need a boyfriend right now, but if it's that important to you, find a decent boy who wants to watch a film." He raises his eyebrows at this and points to himself because he has learned to sit through a chick-flick and because maybe, just maybe, he understands how much I need this. "Go MaccyD's, and bowling, and share a bloody Coke. You're your own worst enemy, you. Get some friends your own age."

I want to tell him about Ritchie. I want to tell him about the storm and about how boys always let you down, but the words get stuck somewhere deep inside my chest.

I've never told anyone. Not even Cee.

During fifth period double maths, I said I needed to use the bathroom and walked out of the school grounds ducking under the new barrier they'd installed to slow the cars down. I needed to think so I headed straight for the woods, walking on the wrong side of the road by the nice houses and the golf club so I wouldn't bump into anyone. But someone was following me. There were footsteps. Heavy breathing.

I didn't stop. I kept walking through the woods, past my oak tree with the twisted trunk that guarded my bear-wolf, heading towards the park and the children's playground. There'd be people there. Eyes down, school bag pinned to my side, I concentrated on my footsteps, not wanting to fall over a stick or a rock and give my shadow a chance to catch up with me and pounce, but when the path finally opened up and became the top of the hill, and daylight washed over me in stormy-purple, the shadow grabbed my shoulders from behind.

I screamed. "Ritchie!"

He laughed out loud, pleased with himself. "I almost didn't recognise you," he said. "And then I thought to myself, no, Summer will be the only person silly enough to go for a walk in the woods when it's about to chuck it down."

I wasn't sure if he was making fun of me, but he smiled and showed me his neat white teeth and his dark brown eyes. He let go of my shoulders, looked away down the hill and then up towards the charging clouds. It seemed as if he were searching for answers he couldn't find on the ground.

"Race you." He grinned.

Before I could answer he was off, running down the hill.

I didn't hesitate. I chased after him, school bag thumping against my back. Way ahead of me, Ritchie hurdled the iron railings surrounding the playground and jumped onto a swing. Already out of breath I considered my options. He was taller than me, a lot taller than me, and I was carrying a bag loaded with textbooks, and if I got stuck halfway over the fence, not only would it be embarrassingly painful, but it would be the least sexy look in the world. Ever. Before I reached the bottom, I'd decided to go through the gate.

"Jump," he shouted. I saw his mouth move but the sound was stolen by the wind. He pointed at the railings, yelled louder, "JUMP!"

Spur of the moment, I tossed my bag over and attempted to vault the fence with both hands clutching the top bar for support. But I misjudged my upper-body strength and ended up almost horizontal with one leg inside the play area and one still dangling towards the ground, slope-side. I giggled despite being winded. I giggled and all my energy was sapped with the effort of laughing and clinging on to save my embarrassment. Ritchie wasn't just any boy from school. He was Cee's brother. And he was. . . Ritchie.

I didn't see him leap from the swing, but I felt his hands on my arms, felt his chest against mine as he dragged me over the fence and placed me feet first on the grass. My laughter was shocked into submission.

"Silly minx," he said.

I felt like I was the only girl in the history of time to ever be called a minx by the only boy in the world, and a fire exploded inside my chest, heat rising upwards through my neck and face, turning me pink and leaving behind a trail of itchy raised heat bumps that I had to force myself not to scratch.

Ritchie took it all in his stride. "Swings," he said. "Bet I can get highest."

My bag was thrown on to the bark covering the swing area and we swung higher and higher, strangely out of synch, until thunder turned the sky violet and the clouds dirty grey. Neither of us suggested going home. I wanted this moment to never end.

"It's weird you hang around with my sister," he said as we lost momentum.

The darkened sky had thrown shadows onto his face, emphasised his cheekbones, the dark circles under his eyes. If I stared at him all night every night, I thought, I'd never grow bored of the sight of him.

A crash of thunder made us jump. We stared up at the racing clouds.

"I love storms," he said. 'Summer storms—they're the best. They make me feel excited. Bad."

"Bad?"

"Yeah." He grinned. He looked like a little boy, mischievous, cheeky. When he smiled it made *me* feel like the adult, hopeless, doomed. "Like the gods are sending us something dangerous and saying, 'Go, and do something bad. And we'll forgive you because we've done something bad too'."

I laughed. It was a nervous sound. I felt the storm too.

"Don't look at me as if I'm crazy. Close your eyes," he said. "Keep them closed and wait."

I saw the lightning with my eyes closed the way it illuminated my eyelids. I counted the seconds, multiplied the number of seconds between lightning and thunder by ten to work out how close the storm was. I counted to two before the bellow vibrated inside my chest.

"Feel it?" he asked.

"Yeah, I feel it." I felt him too, the nearness of him. I smelled his aftershave, the leather of his jacket. I didn't want the storm to end.

When the rain came it was torrential and we were drenched in seconds. Ritchie hid my school bag inside the climbing tower.

"Come on." He took my hand, and we left the play area, ran out to the cricket field at the bottom of the hill. We lifted our faces to the sky, closed our eyes and caught the rain on our tongues. Then he pulled me close to him and kissed me.

He was right. The storm was dangerous. We were dangerous. Fired up and crazy with bad energy gifted to us by the gods, we clung to one another on the wet grass, saturated, drunk on rain and thunder and lightning.

This time it was different. Special. Ritchie didn't tell me what to do, or keep his eyes closed, or wait for me to climb on top of him. He loved me. He held me tight, squeezed my arms and my waist and my hips until they hurt. But I didn't complain. I wanted it to hurt. I wanted to drown in the wet grass and suffocate in his kisses and never have to wake up.

After, we huddled inside the children's climbing tower shivering, suddenly cold.

"This is your storm," he said, brushing a sodden strand of hair from my cheek. "A summer storm for my Summer."

My heartbeat was like wings against glass. *My Summer.*

"I love you," I told him. "I've always loved you."

He held me close, my face nestled against his neck, and stroked my arm.

The next day he was waiting for me outside the school gates. But some year 7 kid elbowed me in the ribs, and when I turned back from punching him in the arm, Ritchie was wrapped around another girl's shoulders.

I don't tell Mac any of these things. He's hung up on being underage, and making something of my life, and he wouldn't understand.

Instead, I tell him I miss Cee the way I'd miss my own heart and he slips an arm around my shoulders and holds me.

17

"You, missy," says Mum when she comes home. "You are going to buy yourself a new outfit cos you'll never guess what I found out tonight."

"Wait for it, Summer. *Hollyoaks* is coming to town." Mac stands with Jonah in his arms and gives Mum a kiss on the cheek.

"Idiot," she says. "No, Courtney's family are planning a lantern ceremony, you know where they let off those candle lantern things." She waves a hand in the air dismissing any need to elaborate. "They're raising money at the same time for the British Heart Foundation. Like her mother won't want to keep it for herself."

I ignore the last comment. "So why am I buying a new outfit?"

"Because you're going." She shakes the question out of her head. In her eyes the candles are already lit, and I'm already there in a new top, and my makeup done like it's a girl's night out at the Leisure Park.

Mac steps back into the room with a bottle wrapped in a tea towel. "Who's sending the invites?"

"What does that matter? Probably no one. You don't need an invite to go and stand in a fucking field."

"Liz," Mac says, sitting back down. "It's not your decision who goes or doesn't go. Where did you even hear this?"

"They were best friends." She points at me so there's no mistake. She's stretched tight with it; one ping and she'll snap.

Mac places a bib on the baby's chest, and I fasten the Velcro at the back of his neck, my fingers brushing Mac's arm. He doesn't notice.

"So, she doesn't need to light a lantern to prove a point. Or she can let one off in the back garden if it's that frigging important."

"Watch my lips," she says. "If everyone is letting off a lantern at the top of a hill to remember my daughter's friend, then my daughter is going to be there, if it's the last thing I do."

She says this like she's doing it for me, like Mac is standing in the way of her claiming the 'Mother of the Year' title, when what she's really doing is scoring points. If she cared about how I feel, she'd have asked me if I needed to go. I check out Tia's Instagram. Her story is a picture of a Chinese lantern and she's tagged the Ovary. I click through to the Ovary's profile and her latest post:

Courtney's send off - lighting up the sky with her friends.

And the first comment:

All the people who loved her will be there.

The first note lands like a whisper on top of the TV licence reminder, and the British Red Cross envelope containing bookmarks and a flimsy blue biro. I watch it land on my way to the kitchen for a can of Diet Coke, notice the silhouette through the glass, even subconsciously register that this correspondence didn't arrive via the postman. But letters are not my thing, so I don't pick them up. I don't get post.

Mum is in the shower. I take the drink back to the living room, get Jonah out of the Moses basket and lay him on this teddy-gym thing that he has; it's furry underneath and has toys dangling from an overhead frame so he can watch them moving or even try to bat them with his hands and feet. I crinkle a butterfly above his face, but he only has eyes for me. I try to remember the words to nursery rhymes from when I was little, but a few minutes pass before it dawns on me that he can't hear them, so I unclip a rattle and wave it above him. He seems to like the colours.

The more I research about my baby brother, at night when I'm in bed, the freer he becomes. His entrapment in his silent world is also his liberty. The real difference with Jonah, and this isn't something I've found on the internet, is that he's in our world but we'll never be in his. So, in my mind I view him inside a perfect transparent bubble, a membrane that's there to protect him from harm.

And I love him for it.

The shower clicks off downstairs and my insides droop the way they used to in year 7 when Mr Davies was late for science class and, just as I psyched myself up for a free period involving no experiments for me to cock up, he'd leap through the door and yell at Sage McBride to get back to her desk. I hear the squirt of hair products, the bathroom door opening. Mum'll sit in front of her dressing table mirror with a towel wrapped around her head, smooth cream into the lines across her forehead, empty a quarter of her wardrobe before she finds something she wants to wear. And it's not like anyone's even going to see her. There's only me and Jonah until Mac gets home from work.

Sometimes I wish Jonah would scream, an ear-shattering, horror-movie kind of scream, just to see her reaction.

She heads upstairs, barefoot, and I sing to Jonah anyways, 'Incy Wincy Spider' and I make my fingers crawl along his legs to tickle his tummy. I want her to come in and see us. I want her to ask what I'm doing, because it'll mean she's thinking about us instead of what she'll wear when she goes to the pub, or how many calories she'll burn on the bike.

"Are they fucking kidding me?" I hear from the top of the stairs. The front door opens. And slams shut again. "Summer! Where did this come from?" She comes into the living room waving a sheet of paper with bold black writing scrawled unevenly across it. Her face is pale. Her chest is heaving like she ran around the block.

"What is it?" I shrug like I don't care, but something about the letters on the page, about how this note came through the letterbox without an envelope, is turning my insides.

"Read it!" She flings the paper at me and it floats prettily down onto Jonah's legs. I see the words before I touch it.

STAY AWAY! YOU'RE NOT WANTED.

I take it off Jonah, hands trembling; I don't want him poisoned by it. There's no doubt in my mind what this is about: it's a warning for us to stay away from Cee's lantern ceremony.

"Who do they think they are?" Mum is shrieking now. The towel is on the floor and she's pacing in and out of the room, footsteps thudding across the carpet. She opens the door a second time and closes it again. "I'm not having this. They can't stop us with a pathetic bloody note." She flings a hand up in the air. "What they gonna do about it? Eh? How they gonna stop us? I'll call the police, that's what I'll do. I'm not having this."

"Mum," I squeeze in between her rants. "MUM!"

Her body stops pacing but her eyes continue to rove, and I imagine her hair like a tangle of snakes writhing in tune to her temper.

"I'm not going anyways," I say.

She stops dead, eyes wide, and the smoothed lines on her forehead return with a vengeance. "You're not staying away because of this." She points at the paper in my hand.

"I said I wasn't going. I don't need to go."

There's so much I could say about how I don't need to send a lantern up into the sky to remember my best friend, about how she still stays with me at night, her body pressing against mine under the duvet, her hands fiddling with my hair the way she always used to, about how she's still the one I talk to when something is on my mind. But I say nothing. Mum's never been interested in what happened that night. She never asks how I feel, whether I'm sad, or lonely, or missing Cee. She has somehow made it all about her, about being vocal, about proving we were the only people who ever cared about Cee.

"I'm not going," I repeat.

Her face sharpens, eyes narrowed. "You. Are. Going," she says slowly. "You're going to get dressed up, do your face, set off a lantern with the rest of them, and you're going to smile while you're doing it. And they can shove *that* up their arses and smoke it."

I'm downstairs in my room when Mac comes home that night. "Throw it in the bin," I hear him say. "Throw it in the bin and forget about it."

"Why should I?" She's had two cans of Stella and about a hundred cigarettes since The Bastards pushed the note through the letterbox. "You think it's okay to threaten people now?"

"I'm not saying that." Mac is covered in plaster-dust and paint from the new-builds he's working on and there are sweat rings under his armpits. He swipes his T-shirt over his head and wipes his face and the back of his neck with it. He looks tired. Mum would normally wait for him to get in the shower before starting but tonight she's too rattled to care. "All I'm saying is leave it. Let the kid rest in peace."

"I'm not the one stirring ashes." For someone with a permanently husky voice she's starting to sound more like Bette Midler in *Hocus Pocus*. "They know Summer should be there, fuck knows she did more—"

"Stick another record on, Liz!" Mac snaps. "This isn't about who did what. This is about a mother saying goodbye to her daughter. How do you think you'd feel?"

Standing behind my door I sense the hesitation, knowing they're probably both staring down the stairs because I'm down here. Cee, sitting at my dressing table brushing her hair, refuses to meet my eyes. We both know it's impossible for Mum to know how it feels, because I'm the one who's still alive. The pills didn't kill me.

A door slams. A dish or mug or plate or something crashes against the kitchen floor before the door bounces off the wall on its way open again.

"You know what?" she screeches. "You take everyone else's bloody side. Don't you worry about us, we'll sort ourselves out, you selfish fucking arsehole." She thumps downstairs and screams at him from her bedroom, "You like 'em that much why don't you take your stuff and go live with them."

"Yeah, it's me who's selfish. I'm not the one throwing your daughter out there to be eaten by the wolves."

I glance at Cee. Her family are the wolves Mac is referring to and I feel guilty because that's down to me too. Mac's trying to protect me from Cee's family, because I'm vulnerable, but what about them? Aren't they vulnerable right now, too? I don't want my best friend to start hating me . . . not now . . .

She winks at me. "Don't worry. I'm not going anywhere."

18

"Remember how your school uniform was different to everyone else's?" We're listening to Drake in my bedroom. It's stuffy and I'm thirsty, but I don't want to go upstairs to the kitchen because they're quiet and I don't want the arguments to start again. Cee is restless tonight like she knows this is all about her.

I nod. "My mum said knee length skirts were ugly and those stupid school socks you had to buy from the school office didn't stay up anyways."

"I was jealous. My skirts were from Primark, and they weren't even the right colour."

I consider telling her about the time Mum kept me home from school when I was put on uniform detention; she told the headmaster I'd achieve more wearing my short skirts and low-neck blouses in school, than I would being stuck at home on detention watching *Loose Women*. But she's already heard this story; it's one of Mum's favourites. I know when other girls in my year were getting Wii-Dance for their birthdays, or in Cee's case some glittery jeans from Primark, I was getting holographic acrylics and going with Mum to get my eyebrows threaded. Cee said I was lucky because there was only me. But now there isn't only me, I don't even feel like I'm here.

"Your skirts were cute," I say.

"You're such a bad liar," Cee says.

We both laugh. Cee snakes an arm around me, and I breathe in the smell of her. So much of her stuff is still here, pyjamas, her black off-the shoulder top and silver belly top, some shorts and heels and perfume which she stole from the Ovary. Marc Jacobs Daisy. Her favourite.

I close my eyes to the humming of the exercise bike in the room above. Mac must be watching the football with Jonah snuggled up in the safety of his arm, a can of beer on the floor by his ankle, the remote on the arm of the sofa. Jonah's eyes will be closed, his lashes, long and gold like mine, like dandelion fluff against his cheek.

It's funny because I've lived in this house since I was a baby. I ate food in front of the telly, in a highchair with a shiny plastic seat, a circle of dolls watching CBeebies with me. I've slept in a Minnie Mouse room, a princess room, a flower kingdom, a One Direction movie set, Grandad with a pencil permanently tucked behind one ear and paint splattered jeans, cup stained with tea and Gran tutting from the doorway, muttering under her breath, "Could he get much bleeding slower?"

And yet I don't feel like I belong here the way Mac and Jonah do.

My phone pings.

Can I come and stay? They've gone away and locked me out. X

Bastards! X. Bring KFC and I'll let you in. X

Now I have to go upstairs and ask them if it's okay and my

stomach is twisting. I wouldn't normally bother, but after Mac's reaction last time I can't deal with another fight.

Mum is flinging tiny droplets of anger onto the floor and her thighs, the front of her vest already saturated. She doesn't stop pedalling. Mac has one leg on the sofa, the other foot on the floor, and the baby is nestled against him between his legs, eyes wide open. It's the first time I've seen his eyes this wide; I hadn't realised how dark they are like a stormy night, like so much knowledge is unravelling behind his eyelids and the storm is a barrier, protection from the outside world. From us. His arms and legs jolt when I walk in and he rolls his head from side to side.

"Hey, baby," I say, and crouch on the floor in front of them, offering him my little finger.

The bike's wheels hum louder.

It's several seconds before I realise my hand is nudging Mac's thigh and I move it away as my cheeks grow hot. Mac's been with Mum since I started senior school and it's only now, since Cee, that his face has become a permanent reality to me and not just someone who stays over because he's screwing my mum. It hits me in a flash that I should be nurturing this development rather than being the spoilt, difficult stepdaughter, because maybe he feels the same way too. I nuzzle the baby, but that makes things even more awkward, and now I can't stand up because Jonah has grabbed a handful of hair and is yanking it towards his mouth.

"I'm stuck," I say.

Mac laughs. "Let go of Summer's hair." He tries to prise open Jonah's fingers, but they only seem to latch on tighter and closer to my roots. How can he be so strong?

My cheek is against Mac's leg and I can smell shower gel, and baby, and fabric softener, and my cheeks sting more than my scalp. I push against him with my hands to stop my face from being buried in Mac's crotch, and the whole thing is so crazy-silly, that giggles force their way up from my chest and out through my smile. Once I start, I can't stop. And because I'm giggling my arms give up the fight against the strongest baby in the world.

Mac is giggling too; I feel his legs shaking against my face as he sits forward and yanks my hair from Jonah's hand. I flop onto the floor, laughing till my cheeks ache, no longer able to feel the sting of wrenched hair roots, or the shame of burying my face against my stepdad's crotch.

The wheels have stopped whirring. Mum is swigging water from a bottle, face pink and clammy, eyes narrowed at the ceiling like she's being forced to watch a couple of kids messing around when she's got far more important things to do.

Mac holds the baby up above his head. "Look what you've done to your sister," he says, his voice still light with laughter.

But my giggles have vanished. I pull my dressing gown across my chest and twist around on to my knees, reaching for Jonah's fingers to hide my embarrassment. "Can Kofi come round?" I ask. "His mum and stepdad have gone away and locked him out of the house."

The fun drains out of the room like a sink emptying.

Mac's mouth is a straight line. "Best ask your mum. She calls the shots."

"They're arseholes," she says. "Course he can come. Maybe he'll talk some sense into you." She raises her eyebrows at Mac as if daring him to challenge her, but he swings his leg

127

off the sofa and goes to the kitchen with Jonah, and I feel her disappointment through the tapping of her foot on the carpet.

19

We eat KFC in bed. I breathe in the smell of chicken and red sauce, and smother the memories of us, me and Cee, in McDonald's, when we rubbed the kids' balloons on our hair and giggled as it pointed upwards and outwards like fine needles, crazy with static.

"Your stepdad won't go mental again, will he?" Kofi asks, sucking grease from his thumb.

"Shh." I point to the wall opposite the bed. "He's in there."

"What's going on? This house feels like mine but without the fakery. How was your day, darling?" he raises his voice till he sounds like a cartoon character, a kind of Jessica Rabbit. "I cooked your steak just the way you like it, and tomorrow I'll scrub the toilet with my toothbrush to make you happy." I think I prefer it this way, like climbing an icy mountain rather than being spoon-fed poisoned sugar." He keeps his eyes on the food, so I don't see the hurt.

"What are you going to do?"

He shrugs. "I'll either walk out one day or I'll kill him." He's not smiling. He's serious.

I picture his stepdad with blue lips and vacant eyes, tucked inside a blue plastic bag, and it quickly morphs into Cee, bubbly happy beautiful Cee who would've hated having her face covered with plastic and being tipped onto a cold marble slab. I can't eat any more.

"Don't kill him, you'll go to jail."

"Ha! I'll plead crime of passion or something, and you can stand up in court and give me a character reference." I toss my chicken into the box and tuck the lid back in. "Do you have to go to court about Cee?" he asks.

"Maybe. Yes. You know what my mum's like. She's told them I've been through enough without having to stand up in a room full of suits and wigs and relive the whole thing. I'm fragile apparently. Apart from when I'm strong. Depends on what mood they're in. I'll have to give evidence about the accident and tell them that Cee brought the pills." I swallow after I say the words aloud. It's going to sound like I'm lying in court to save myself, when even Tia thinks that it was me.

As if we're somehow connected telepathically, a Snapchat comes through from Tom. It's the first time I've heard from him since the accident. My hands are shaking. I feel hot and cold like my blood doesn't know how to react. Do I patch it?

"What?" Kofi asks. "What is it?"

"A snapchat . . . from Tom. The guy who—the guy whose car we were in."

"Open it," Kofi says gently. "I'm here."

Make sure you tell everyone I had nothing to do with those pills.

Kofi must see it in my eyes because he peers at my phone over my shoulder. "Bastard. He knows he's going down for being caught out with underage girls in his car."

"Nothing happened," I whisper.

"Doesn't matter, Summer. He's a grown man who should know better. The intention was there, believe me."

I know he's right. I knew it when I climbed out of the top window to go and meet him.

"You'll walk into that court and you'll tell the truth. No one can prove that you gave them to her."

"What if he lies and says that he saw me do it?"

"It'll be your word against his, and he's hardly a reliable witness. You were her best friend. He's some slimeball from Upminster." Kofi stuffs about twenty French fries into his mouth in one go and shifts his shoulders from side to side while he studies me.

"You pig," I say. I can't help smiling at his bulging cheeks but now I can't help thinking that Tom is going to lie about what happened and I'm scared.

"What can I say? I'm starving." He swallows, tips the carton up so the remaining chips slide into his mouth. Munching and swallowing, he says, "I don't think you're fragile or strong."

"So, what do you think I am?"

"Dunno." He shrugs. "You haven't worked it out yet neither."

Tears spring from nowhere, clinging to my eyelashes and I turn away from him, and pretend to tidy away the food boxes. When Cee was here, I knew who I was: I was her best friend and she was mine. I didn't have to pretend with Cee. If I wanted to slob out in last night's jammies all day and eat a whole box of Jaffa cakes while I watched *Made in Chelsea* on catch up, she'd fetch a family sized bag of Walkers cheese and onion, and a water bottle filled with gin, and join me. If I felt like getting wasted and kipping on Tia's sofa for twenty-four hours, she'd do that too. She'd hold my hair when I was sick and hold my hand when my heels gave me blisters. No one else would do that.

"If you want my opinion," Kofi says. "And you probably don't, I'd dump these pals of yours."

"You mean Tia and Frankie?"

"Yeah, they don't smile right?"

"What do you mean?" I slump back on my pillow and tuck my dressing gown around me like I'm a mummy.

"I mean, they're not your friends. They might act like they are, but when it comes down to it, they'll be the first ones pointing the finger in your direction if you're ever in trouble."

I think about the beauty salon and the way they all studied their toenails when the woman mugged me off. I've only heard from Tia when she wanted money for the hen weekend, and I know they've been out without me because I've seen the photos on Facebook.

"But they were Cee's friends too."

"And your point is?"

"I don't know."

What was my point? If Cee liked them, I should like them too? I'd never questioned it. Cee hung around with them because they got her into pubs. They hung around with Cee because she was fun to be around. Or at least that's what I believed. I think back to nights out, sparkly tops and six-inch heels, false eyelashes peeling from the side of the bathroom sink the following morning, too many perfumes clinging to the duvets and cushions. Tia, drunk, was really aggy. You had to tiptoe around her or dodge the pair of scissors flying towards your left eye. She couldn't deal with Bliss when she had a hangover, so Cee used to feed her Weetabix, sit on the floor, and build towers from plastic blocks and read stories to her: *The Gruffalo* and *We're Going on a Bear Hunt*, battered ex-library copies that someone had given her. And we'd all taken the mick out of her, said she'd end up being the Ovary junior.

"Cee didn't have a choice," Kofi says, as if reading my mind. "She was escaping in the only way she knew how, by hanging out with older women. She had to be the grown up at home, so she might as well be the grown up outside."

"No, she hated looking after her brothers and sister."

"Precisely my point. Do you have any chocolate? I really need chocolate now."

"You're such a girl," I say.

"Why, thank you."

"But Cee did have a choice," I say, ignoring Kofi's fake hormones. "She chose me."

"So, you have a choice too." He leaves the bed and sits at my dressing table, rummaging through my makeup and studying his reflection in the mirror. The way he sits, back straight and slim legs crossed, he could almost be mistaken for a girl from behind. "You want friends who help you fly, not pile up the baggage."

"Have you been having counselling or something?"

He swivels to face me and winks. "Always, honey."

I can't hear Mum upstairs—she's probably on the veranda having a cigarette and swigging a bottle of cider, checking out her Instagram feed and hitting the like button on The Rock's page.

Before Mac and the exercise bike, there was Brian and his convertible. Sunny days we'd drive out to the coast and cruise along the seafront where Mum could turn her nose up at people from behind her fake Ray-Bans, and pretend her clothes were real designer and not some cheap version shipped over from Asia. Brian had an accent. It didn't matter though because he spoke to me through her, and if I kicked off, he walked away and left us until Mum promised I'd behave.

Before Brian, there were cans of Stella every night, and Johnny with his lazy eye that looked like it couldn't quite wake up. I saw his willy once when he was peeing in the bathroom with the door open. Before that, it was the shopping centre. The manager of the champagne bar called Mum in for a free glass of Prosecco whenever we walked past. She'd slide onto a white stool, and he'd pick me up and sit me down beside her with a plastic glass of sparkly water; special sparkles for a special princess, he'd say. She leaned across the bar and allowed him to stroke the tattoo on her arm, and on the way home she'd sing in the car.

Before that, it was Tommy-boy and Sunday morning football matches with runny noses and scarves making my neck sweaty. And before that, it was *Twilight* and new-Billy—at the same time.

If I set out all the pieces of Mum's life like a jigsaw puzzle, there I am filling in the gaps. Cracks were imperfections, and there could be no cracks for her life to slip through so there was me, clinging to her side like glue waiting for her to stick.

So where did Jonah fit in?

"If you had a choice," Kofi says. "You wouldn't pick Mac for a stepdad, would you?" He uses my eyebrow pencil to tidy up his brows and pouts at me in the mirror. "I mean he's your mum's choice, right?"

"Yeah, I guess."

"Take my stepdad—the uneducated white man who believes I'm a typical badass black boy packed with a knife, so his aim is to break my fingers before I kill someone."

How could anyone be so wrong? Kofi is the sweetest, gentlest boy I've ever known and if he wasn't gay, he'd make a brilliant boyfriend for some lucky girl, some day. His stepdad must view him through someone else's spectacles.

"So, your stepdad?" he says.

The vision of my face shoved in Mac's crotch springs to mind and my cheeks grow hot. When Mac first arrived, I used to listen to his telephone conversations with other women out on the balcony and repeat them word for word to Mum the following day.

"What do you want me to say?" she'd ask, while she was doing her face.

When Mac brought home pizza for dinner, I refused to eat it, even if I was starving and, once, after they had a massive row, he bought me some makeup as an apology; I took it down to my room and used the whole lot in one go, layering my mouth with lipstick until my lips were puffy and sore.

Jonah has changed everything. The baby has painted Mac a lighter shade of stepdad, given him facets that were never on show before, shown me edges that aren't always unbreakable, and if I needed to, I'd speak to Mac before Mum now because he's not the one with the agenda.

This change in dynamics has snuck in through the hole left by Cee, without me even realising, and I wonder if Mum has noticed it too.

Kofi is still watching me through the mirror.

"Well, he's not so bad, I guess," I eventually say.

135

20

It's late morning when we leave my room. Mum's door is open wide, and I can't see Jonah in the Moses basket. Music is blaring from the living room: George Ezra. Cee and I used to sing along to 'Paradise', loudly, and out of tune, and I swallow back tears which are starting to feel like they're permanently clogging my throat.

My head is cloudy with sleep and I'm uncomfortable in my own skin, so we head straight into the kitchen where I fill a bowl with cornflakes and milk for Kofi and switch the kettle on to boil to make coffee. Last night's KFC is still lodged in my chest and I can't eat, but I find the chocolate digestives in the fridge and take them too.

In the living room, the door is open onto the veranda and a breeze flutters the pages of a magazine. On the sofa, Mum sits with Jonah on her lap, feet pointing towards her and his fragile head cradled in one hand, a bottle in her other hand. As usual she looks awkward, unnatural, so unprepared for motherhood like she hasn't already done this once before, and I wonder if she got Gran to do everything for me when I was new-born.

She gives us a half-smile. "You're up."

"Sorry, she kept me talking all night." Kofi digs his elbow into my ribs. "Can I make you a coffee?" He doesn't wait for an answer but dives straight onto his knees, spilling milk onto his shorts, and strokes Jonah's head. "Hey, little bro, is that your breakfast?" His voice is so light I imagine it floating away out of the window and across the treetops.

"It's lunchtime actually," Mum says. "I don't know what to do with him today. He doesn't want to go down and I'm supposed to be covering Jamal in the shop."

I think she doesn't know what to do with him any day, but I keep quiet and sip my coffee. She's the mum here.

"We'll look after him," offers Kofi. He glances up at me with his wide brown eyes and his still perfect eyebrows. "Eh? We're not doing anything."

"We are now," I say even though I don't mean it and I'd rather she went out and left us with the baby because the eggshells on the carpet disappear when the door closes behind her, and the storm clouds in the air transform into a sunny summer day. I give attitude because I don't want to make it easy for her.

I needn't have bothered though. She twists the bottle out of Jonah's still sucking mouth and holds him at arm's length.

"Which one of you wants to finish the feed?" She's on her feet and smiling, like she doesn't even attempt to conceal her elation at being released.

"I'll do it," Kofi says with a mouthful of cornflakes and milk trickling down his smooth chin. He sets the bowl onto the coffee table and takes Jonah into the crook of his arm.

They look so cute together, Kofi's dark skin and Jonah's pale creamy face, that I can't help but smile.

"I need a picture," I say, whipping my phone out of my dressing gown pocket. "Smile."

Mum is out the door with a waft of J-Lo Glow and a flash of red lipstick. "You know what you're doing," she says to me. "I should be home about the same time as Mac."

"That's convenient," I say to Kofi.

"We'll be fine," Kofi calls out too late.

He holds Jonah upright against his shoulder and rubs his back to wind him. "What? It'll be fun," he says. "Hey, little fella. You want to listen to your Uncle Kofi singing musicals, eh?"

"Kofi, he can't hear you properly, remember?" I whisper.

"No but you can, and he can see, can't he? I'll be flamboyant, darling." He waves an arm in the air like he's Freddie Mercury or John Barrowman. "And crazy, and I'll dance."

Jonah sleeps for a while and we watch Netflix, and Kofi tells me about the drama classes he's been attending at a proper drama studio in town, where some actor who played Puck in *A Midsummer Night's Dream* at the Globe, studied. I don't know anything about *A Midsummer Night's Dream* other than it's Shakespeare, but Kofi is excited. His face glows when he speaks about Puck; I wonder if he fancies him.

"The bastard won't let my mum take me though," he says trying on my chiffon kimono from last summer. "What do you think of this?" He swings his arms and the gauzy material floats and settles around him.

"It suits you. What do you mean? Take you where?"

"To drama school. I have to walk or get a lift back with someone else if they offer, and if it's gone nine o'clock, I've had it. Door locked. Dinner in the bin. Cha feel?" He slips off the kimono and pulls from the wardrobe a floor length silver cardigan. "Summer, this is cute."

"What do you do if it's late then? I mean . . . what do you do?"

He shrugs. "Kip on my mate's floor if he's sober. One time I sat in McDonald's till it shut. I ate a chip every ten minutes to drag it out, then I went to the park. I slept a bit under the slide, but it gets cold when you're not moving, so I got up and kept walking until I knew he'd gone to work."

"Why doesn't your mum tell him to go fuck himself?"

He smiles. "Probably because he'd go fuck someone else, and then come back and fuck her."

"I don't get why she stays with him," I say. "Choices, remember—why does she choose him?"

"Why does anyone choose anyone? Because they're scared of the alternative. Right, I'm ready." Kofi twirls in the silver cardigan and denim shorts and he looks so much like the little boy in reception class that I want to punch his stepdad in the throat.

Upstairs, Jonah's arms are punching the air above the Moses basket.

"You feed him, and I'll find the movie. I know what I'm looking for." Kofi searches for, and finds, *The Greatest Showman*.

"Really?" I say.

"Uh-huh. If you haven't watched it, you haven't lived."

So, I warm Jonah's bottle, settle into Mac's corner of the sofa and prepare to live. And the boy can sing. I mean he really can sing, and these are proper belters. I sit Jonah on my lap facing Kofi in the middle of the living room so he can watch, and he is so mesmerised I start to wonder if he's been fooling us all along and there's nothing wrong with his hearing. We're on our second movie screening, and my cheeks are aching from smiling like I've been posing for wedding photographs, and I'm clapping Jonah's hands at the end of 'From Now On', when Mac walks in.

Kofi stops singing and his hands drop to his sides, chest heaving because he's been a proper ballerina, leaping and dropping to his knees, and pretending to chase a train like Hugh Jackman.

"What's going on?" Mac asks. He squints like he's confused.

"Kofi's been singing for Jonah," I say, before he can get angry. "He's been loving it." I clap the baby's hands to prove my point, and Jonah smiles for the first time. "Oh my God! He's smiling."

Mac drops to his knees by the sofa and plants a kiss on Jonah's forehead. "He's smiling," he says.

His eyes are moist as they meet mine, his thumb tracing a circle round and around the back of my hand, and my chest swells because I feel responsible for making our baby happy.

I glance up at Kofi above Mac's head, and he glances away quickly as if he's been watching something he shouldn't have seen.

"Come on then, let's hear you sing," Mac says. He sits on the floor beside us.

"Yeah, come on, Kofi. See if you can make him smile again," I say.

I'm desperate to preserve the warm and happy feeling from this moment because suddenly it feels like I haven't been warm and happy in forever, and I don't want Kofi to stop singing, because when he stops, I know I'll feel guilty all over again for smiling without my best friend by my side.

Kofi rewinds the movie to 'Rewrite the Stars,' and pretends he's flying on a trapeze as he sings. The baby kicks his legs, and I don't know who I should watch the most.

"He's good," Mac whispers, with a nod in Kofi's direction. I force a smile, clinging to the moment.

Before I can answer, we hear Mum outside the front door, or rather we hear her shouting. The whole town must hear her shouting.

"You must be some stupid bitch thinking you'll get away with this. You try and stop us!"

21

Kofi's face pales if that's at all possible; his mouth drops.

Mac closes his eyes briefly and rubs his hand across the back of his neck. "Stay there," he says, standing slowly.

The key turns in the lock. There's another voice outside I recognise as the Ovary, but I only catch a few words being screamed in retaliation, "Killed my daughter!'

"She can't even drive, you fucking idiot!"

Kofi dives onto the sofa beside me, as Mac says, "Liz, come inside, come on."

"I'm calling the police right now!" Mum yells. "Stay there, you can watch me do it!" She laughs out loud, but the sound is more a cackle, and I can almost picture her wild black hair flying above a broomstick.

"Liz! Leave it, will you? Before it's too late."

The door slams shut, and I know she's inside; I can hear her breathing. Instinctively I clutch Jonah closer to me and realise he's asleep. I wish I could do that. I wish I could sleep through the raised voices, and the accusations that'll probably continue way into the night, only to be followed by sulking and nasty digs at each other, until Mac relents and spends some money on her.

"I thought our house was bad," whispers Kofi. "She's a Rottweiler."

"Pit bull," I say. We would laugh if we weren't both so scared that she'll turn on us.

I think I know why Grandad puts up with Gran: he's probably scared of her too. I can imagine Mum raging around their house as a teenager, slamming doors and destroying clothes until she got what she wanted. She dropped out of college and ran away with my dad to Cornwall because he was a surfer, and she loves the sun. I only know this because whenever we watch a film with someone surfing, she always says, "Your dad would've smashed that," or, "Your dad was better looking than him."

When she came back with me and without a man, Grandad bought her this house so she could go back to college, but then she fell in love with a tattoo artist who taught her how to do piercings.

"Put your phone away," Mac speaks quietly but firmly.

"Don't tell me what to do, Mac." From the sofa, I imagine her in the hallway, shrugging him off. "This is not okay. She can't go around sending threatening letters to people."

"Her daughter just died for Christ's sake."

"Ugh!" There's a crash and the sound of something smashing.

"Liz, come on, sweetheart. This isn't achieving anything." Mac is cajoling now, the way he speaks to Jonah.

"Get off me."

"You're letting them win this way." I wonder if Mac is holding her head against his chest, stroking her hair, because we can hear her crying. "This is exactly what they want. You've got to be the bigger person and let it go."

143

"She's not getting away with this." Footsteps. The front door opens again. "I'm coming for you, you fat slag!"

Kofi and I both stare at the living room door like we might see through it but keep them out at the same time. The front door slams and Mac peers into the living room and says, "Stay with the baby for a bit, yeah?" and is gone.

He bundles her downstairs, and they go quiet.

Kofi and I talk in whispers.

"Is she always this angry?" he says.

"Pretty much." I shrug. "It's because she isn't getting her own way. This is all over the lantern ceremony. I don't even know why it's so important to her."

"This is for Cee?"

"Yeah, it's just letting off some lanterns."

I study Jonah's perfect pout with his face squashed up against my chest and I wonder if she misses him when she goes out all night, or does she deliberately force him out of her mind? Has she ever missed me when I stay out? No questions are ever asked; it's simply taken for granted I'm okay because I made it back home. Cee is only ever mentioned when she's talking about funeral arrangements, and lantern flipping ceremonies, and her 'bloody mother' talking to reporters. It's almost as if grief is measured by how many people see your sadness. The more you cry in public, the more hurt you must be.

Suddenly I wish I'd never posted my Facebook status. I think none of this would be happening if I'd kept my mouth shut.

"I miss her," I say to Kofi.

He wraps his arms around me, around me and the baby, and holds us tightly. "I know you do," he whispers. "I know you do. No one can replace her, she was your best friend and she's left a big fat hole in your chest, but . . ."

He takes a deep breath as though he's psyching himself up for some great reveal that'll shock the pants off me. I hold my breath too. I'm not sure I want to hear it, because I think I know where he's going with this. All the moments I would've filled with Cee, I've been spending with Jonah and Mac, thinking that they'll always be here to pick me up when I'm down. And what if they're not?

"I'm here if you need someone to talk to. Talk to me, Summer. Please."

Big fat tears crawl out of the corners of my eyes, dripping off the end of my chin and on to Kofi's arms, splashing like raindrops. I cry properly for the first time since the accident, because it's the first time since the accident that anyone has spoken about Cee in this way. And because I know he's right. I can't fill the hole in my chest with someone else. The hole is my reminder of our friendship—I need it to keep Cee with me.

He talks through my sobs quietly and gently. "I might not look good in a pink playsuit, but I sure can carry off a floral polo. I'll prop up the bar with you when you can't face it alone. And hell, why not, I'll even sing karaoke with you, so long as you choose a little old Sam Smith number. I'll tell you when you look beautiful. And I'll tell you when you don't." He pauses. "What else does a bestie do?"

I peer at him through strands of damp hair. "Lend me a tampon." I sniff out a kind of smile.

"See now you're talking." He strokes my hair. "What's a tampon?"

145

A giggle struggles its way out of my tear-clogged throat as we hear the letterbox flap thud closed.

"Stay there." Kofi eases his arms away from us and holds up a finger. He leaves us with a rush of cooling air and pads along the hallway to the front door. He isn't smiling when he returns. "Summer, there's something rank and smelly sitting on the mat."

We don't tell her.

Whatever Mac has promised has worked, because the next morning she is all smiles, and bed-hair, and singing out of tune to Beyoncé while she fries bacon and eggs for him. "Do you two want bacon rolls?" she calls out when we finally surface.

I can't eat. The stink of poo still lingers upstairs, even though Kofi scrubbed the mat and bleached the kitchen sink after he disposed of it. The boy has OCD. I haven't even mentioned the TikTok clips going around of the Chinese lanterns from *Tangled* and people saying, "I'm letting off a lantern for Courtney."

Mac is in the kitchen making up bottles for Jonah. The bits of her smashed phone litter the counter which means Gran will be round to take her to Carphone Warehouse and get her a replacement. Mac, tea towel slung over his shoulder, glances round when we appear.

"There they are," he says. "The Thompson twins."

Kofi raises his eyebrows at me. I shrug. Sometimes Mac can be a right freak.

"That's gone way over your heads, hasn't it?" Mac says, more to himself than anyone else.

Mum laughs. "I'm not surprised."

It's been so long since her mood has been this easy. A few

weeks ago, I'd have wished I could capture it in a bottle and sprinkle it around whenever we needed it, because even from behind she seems softer, more spreadable butter than burnt toast.

"Kofi's coming on Tia's hen weekend," I say. We decided last night over *The Princess Switch*, but as soon as the announcement is made, I wish I'd kept quiet.

She stops splashing eggs in the pan and frowns at us over her shoulder. "That's a great idea. I was going to say I'll come too. Mac will be here with the baby."

Mac has stopped buttering slices of bread. He glances up, shakes his head at me.

My heart starts rousing little butterflies inside my chest. "I don't know," I say. "There was one space."

Course there was one space. It's Cee's space. She knows that, and the way she jumped on the opportunity it seems she's been planning all along to invite herself last minute. I try to imagine her there, dancing with her eyes closed, fingers pointing up at the disco ball like she's at a rave. She'll be slaughtered. She'll be loud. I remember at her cousin's wedding when she disappeared outside and left me with Auntie Rita and her snotty grandchildren Lola and Freda who wanted me to dance the Macarena with them. When Mum came back her jacket had white stuff on the sleeve and her mascara had streaked under her eyes.

If she comes, it'll be all about her. Tia and the others won't care; they'll all be off their faces. They'll encourage her. Tia's mum will be there too; she has a tongue piercing and tiny eyes that she rims with black eyeliner, and when she stares at you it's best not to stare back. I've seen her in a fight. I've seen

147

her drag a girl through the Tavern by her hair and spit on her outside and my mum doesn't know when to keep her mouth shut. It'll be carnage.

I don't want her to come. For the first time ever, I want to do this without her. Behind her, Mac is still shaking his head.

She must see me glance at him because she whirls on the spot, hair flying and feral, and snaps, "Don't tell her what to do. I'm definitely going now."

Just once, I think, just one time can't she think about how I feel?

22

Kofi comes with me to the park. I don't know why I hadn't thought of it before, but it was like I was too scared to be the me I was with Cee, too scared to show my face because I had no place there without her.

They are all there, Ritchie and his mates. It feels like stepping into a parallel universe where life has proceeded as normal, where they still have a crate of beer on the grass in the middle of a haphazard circle of bodies and bikes, where the sun is still shining on them, and the grass still gets damp overnight. It's wrong. How can they still come here and not miss the hole Cee left in the world the night she died?

"Let's go," I say to Kofi.

"Summer don't give up before you've even started. You have as much right to be here as they do. One question—that's all you want to ask. One simple question and then we'll be on our way, and you're one step closer to spilling to the cops. You can't go to them with a bucketful of nothing but other people's attempts to pin this on you."

I nod. I've spotted Ritchie with his bike. I'm not sure if he's noticed me yet, but he's bound to notice Kofi in his yellow tie-dyed T-shirt and black skinny jeans.

As we get closer, Ritchie stops, a can of lager raised halfway to his lips, and his eyes narrow. He tosses the can aside and straddles his bike.

"Ritchie!" I yell.

But he races up the hill towards the trees, glancing over his shoulder at us as though we might be following him.

We keep walking until we reach the circle of boys.

"Summer?" One calls, his face screwed up as if he can't be sure that it's really me. "Are you okay?"

I nod, tears swimming in my eyes, because I didn't expect him to ask about me. "I wanted to speak to Ritchie."

His gaze takes in the bike now at the top of the hill. "Yeah, I don't think he wants to speak to you."

"I need to speak to him about Cee. About that night."

The boy takes a deep breath and stares at his trainers. "Yeah, like I said, I don't think that's a good idea."

"Look, all I want to know is where Cee got the pills from. That's all." My eyes are pleading with him to look at me and help me.

His eyes flit between me and Kofi. "Who's this?"

"Kofi." I glance at Kofi standing beside me. "He's my friend. Do you know where she got them? Does Ritchie know? Did one of you get them for her?"

"Yeah, I think you should go." He raises himself to his full height, which still isn't as tall as Kofi. "Why would I tell you that?"

"Because I'm being blamed for something I didn't do." Tears are streaming down my face now and dripping onto my chest, but his face is expressionless, his eyes cold. I glance at the pile of stuff in the middle of the circle and there's a tiny polythene packet chucked on top of a can of Bud.

I don't hesitate. I run towards the circle, but the boy is fast. He catches me easily, his arms reaching around my waist from behind, and drags me away from the other kids, my legs thrashing the air.

Kofi reaches us, and Ritchie's mate shoves me onto the floor and faces him. "Yeah, you wanna start, do you?" His fists are clenched by his sides.

"No," Kofi says, his voice even. "What you just did—that was assault. And I'm her witness."

"Ha! And which cop's gonna take her side?" He shoots me a look that is worse than the lump of poo landing on the mat by the front door.

Kofi helps me to my feet. I'm crying, and I can't even look at them because I know they're all staring at me. Of course they blame me. Who else is there to blame?

The threats don't stop there. A dead bird, its wing pulverised and bloody, is pushed through the letterbox the following day. I'm glad Kofi is still here because I can't pick it up. Mac says it's best not to tell Mum—what she doesn't know won't hurt her, and their boat's rocky enough since she's insisting on coming to Tia's hen do in Butlin's with us.

The notes I keep, folded up tiny and blunt, in the ballerina jewellery box I've had since I was little. Some are scribbled in black marker that blots the paper through to the other side. Some are written in biro. But they all mean the same thing: No one is going to speak to me.

I jump whenever the letterbox opens. My blood gushes around my head whenever I creep along the hallway to discover the latest warning: a buckled beer can still dribbling liquid, a sticky pink sweetie crawling with ants, a decapitated worm in a tangle of stringy clumpy soil, everything silenced, defeated. Uneasiness has settled around my shoulders like a monochrome cloak, some days greyer than others; it's the first thing I'm aware of when I wake in the mornings, and the last thing I think about before I go to sleep at night. Kofi, when he goes back home, when the arseholes are back from holiday, tells me not to worry. The police, if we decide to tell them, will make them stop; they won't have a leg to stand on and I've done nothing wrong.

He says this gripping my arms tight and staring into my eyes to make me listen.

"You are not a bad person," he says. "One day, when this has all calmed down and her family can sit and think about it rationally, they'll realise you loved Cee too. They'll realise you're heartbroken too. And then they'll be sorry, and you can get your life back on track."

But he's wrong.

Mum still buzzes around with her new iPhone, searching for outfits, holding up pictures of jumpsuits and bodysuits and saying, "How about this one, Summer? Butlin's or lantern?" with a demonic grin like she's stumbled out of a scene from *Corpse Bride*.

I know what she's doing. She thinks if she mentions it often enough, she'll get her own way and I'll go anyways. She's the same when Mac is at home, making little digs and Googling where to buy Chinese lanterns, and how much did he think was reasonable to donate to the British Heart Foundation?

"We don't want her slagging us off for being tight."

Mac rolls his eyes, stares at the telly. "Donate whatever you want. Makes no difference what I say." And she smiles because she's confident she's winning.

In my room I smooth the notes across my bed and read each one in turn.

STAY AWAY BITCH.

NO ONE WANTS YOU.

WHY DON'T YOU CRAWL INTO A HOLE AND DIE?

WE KNOW WHAT YOU DID.

They don't.

I'm the one carrying that bag on my back. Me. And the one person I could talk to about it is gone. Tears well in my eyes as they seem to do every day now, and Cee is behind me whispering, "Told you what she was like, Summer. She's just angry because I'm not there to bring up her kids."

It's not that though; there's more to it than a woman who's had to get up off her backside and look after her own children. This is flaming red anger and it's directed solely at me. Because if Cee and I hadn't been friends, she'd still be here, and Demi and Drew and the new baby, and even Vinny, who I always forget about because he spends more time outside throwing stones at the garages than he does inside, would still have their big sister and the person who cared about them the most.

"Do you miss them?" I ask her.

She turns away and sits at my dressing table so I can only see the mirror version of Cee rather than the real thing. "Yes," she applies pink lip gloss and smacks her lips. "Annoying little turds."

"But you hated looking after them," I say.

"I was a selfish crap-bag." She outlines her eyebrows with my Mac pencil. "I wanted to be like Ritchie. If he could escape and do exactly what he wanted to do with his life, I wanted to be the same. It was unfair. Why should he get away with it and not have her breathing down his neck? I don't miss her, but the kids . . . they deserve better." She flutters her eyelashes and pouts. This would be when our phones came out and we'd take about fifty million selfies trying to get the perfect image where my left eye didn't look lazy, and Cee's spot slap bang in the middle of her nose didn't resemble a volcano. But I don't feel like taking a selfie.

I don't feel like doing anything. I pick up the slip of paper closest to me. I know she's watching me, but today it's hit me like another brutal punch in the stomach, that she's gone, and I can't even look at her beautiful face, I miss her so much. A message interrupts my thoughts. Tia. I hit delete. One thought at a time. Bad enough that I have to go to the hen weekend because I can't let her down, but thoughts of Tia and the others aren't exactly inspiring me to smiles and excitement the way they might've done a few months ago. It was all about the attention. Only attention comes in different forms, I'm starting to realise, and not all of them are healthy.

The writing on the notes is clumsy, the ink smudged like it was left out in the rain or written by someone who was crying. The Ovary isn't someone you'd want to provoke or get on the wrong side of, but when I try to picture her standing in her kitchen with a pen and paper, eyes narrowed and eyebrows pinched with the words she's writing down, I can't. This is premeditated. She might as well stab me in the back and stick a note to me with Blu-tac. But no matter how hard I try, I can't help thinking the Ovary is a smash-your-door-down-think-about-it-later kind of woman. Like my mum. All thunder and no lightning, or however the saying goes that Gran says.

I hold the note to my nose, and I know she didn't do it. There's not a whiff of perfume, not a trace of DKNY or Gucci Bloom, nothing. A glance over my shoulder and Cee's gone. She knows.

She knows who is trying to scare me.

23

She spreads makeup and hair products across the apartment bathroom and doesn't bother unpacking.

"Just zip it back up when we're ready to go," Mum says with a shrug. "If you two are fannying about with hangers and stuff, I'm going to get a drink." She doesn't wait, and as the door slams behind her, I take my first serious breath since we left home and try to ignore the lingering smell of dog food and puke.

"It'll be okay. Two days and we can sleep half of that in a drunken coma," Kofi says.

"Maybe we should wait for her to pass out before we start, you know, like drinking in shifts."

"Or maybe we wait until they're all drunk and we go out in disguise." Kofi holds a shimmering nude mini dress up against his body and twirls. "See, they'd never recognise me."

"Nah but the stubble might be a giveaway."

Driving to Butlin's in the people carrier, I sat at the back in the corner, my face pressed up against the window, and my earphones in listening to Lewis Capaldi and Jorja Smith. Kofi sat next to me. I felt sorry for him, because Mum was the other side of him, and she spent the entire journey leaning across the seat in front, spilling Coke and yelling at them to change the music, because it was a hen weekend they were travelling to, not a fucking wake. I kept my eyes closed. If anyone could deal with her, it's Kofi.

I sit on the end of the bed and it collapses, one loose leg giving and spilling me onto the floor.

"Oops," I say as Kofi, trying not to giggle, gives me a hand up.

"That can be your mum's side. She won't even notice."

"Can I come and live with you?" I ask.

"Baby, stick with what you've got, trust me on this one." He hasn't spoken about what happened when his mum and stepdad got back from their weekend away, but his jaw is swollen, and he turned up this morning with no clothes, not even a carrier bag with some pants slung in, muttering something about cannibalistic terrapins. I don't know what he's going to do. I'd die if I didn't have clean knickers with me, but he's still all white teeth and energy and hanging up my stuff so the room isn't a mess.

"You're such a girl."

"Well, that's the nicest thing you've said to me in ages," he says.

It takes me an age to do my makeup; my eyebrows won't go right, and I feel minging whenever I peer too closely at my reflection in the mirror, all blue veins and dry skin, and hollows beneath my eyes. I haven't eaten, so three drinks and I'll melt into a vodka puddle anyways. Kofi is on the sofa playing on his phone.

"You can go if you want," I say. "Get the drinks in."

He appears leaning against the bathroom door frame,

eyebrows raised. "Not a chance. Someone's got to keep an eye on you."

"I'm not the one who needs watching," I mumble. "Even my bloody eyelashes aren't staying on. Ugh!" I chuck them on the floor and stamp on them with my bare feet.

"I see where you get it from." He laughs and flops back onto the sofa.

Forty-seven minutes later I'm ready. I take a deep breath. Cee should be here getting ready with me—I can't even take a selfie without her because it doesn't feel right. I post one of my favourite pictures of me and Cee on Instagram and say:

Miss you every day xxx

"I don't even want to go," I say to Kofi.

"Look." He holds my hands. "I know what I said about them but, for this weekend, try and pretend they've got your back. We're here now. We might as well enjoy it. And for a couple of days, you can stop worrying about turds dropping through the letterbox, and who's going to light a Chinese lantern or not, and just be you. Okay?" He tucks my hair behind my ears and crushes me against his chest before I ruin my mascara.

I hold in the tears. "You're a turd," I say.

They're on the Woo-woos. Jugs of them. And Mum is on a stool with some guy practically dribbling on her tits. Each time she goes outside for a fag he follows her, his mates cheering him along like he can't do it without back up, and I count the minutes till she comes back, silently expecting her not to come back at all.

They're loud. Tia's wearing a pink plastic tiara and a veil dotted all over with playing cards with pictures of naked men. "Here's my baby girl." She yanks at my shoulder and I feel finger-bruises in the back of my arm as she pulls me close and kisses my cheek. "Love you, Summer."

She's already pissed.

"Love you too, babe." I'm such a fraud. But she's already leaning on Frankie and rubbing her fanny against Frankie's thigh as she dances, and I think it doesn't even matter that I'm a fraud because no one will notice and even if they did notice, they wouldn't give a fuck. I order a vodka shot and down it.

"Bring on Abba!" Kofi downs a shot and orders another two. "My stepdad's paying."

The kiddies' disco is playing 'Baby Shark' and there are mums on the dance floor doing all the actions with their kids while the dads drown in their pints of beer, and wish they were at home playing FIFA. The whole place is filled with people and noise and alcohol stains, and I imagine Jonah at home smelling of baby powder and Mac, his pudgy arms flapping out of his basket, and when I try to think of him as a three-year-old, bouncing his knees and rocking his shoulders along to the music I can't see him on the polished wooden floor.

Mum's off again. She probably hasn't even thought about her baby; she doesn't look like a mum who's wondering if her baby is asleep, or warm, or fed. She looks like a woman on the pull. You see them every weekend over the Leisure Park, sucking up to the bouncers, nicking the lollipops from the bathrooms because they think they look sexy licking it provocatively and sticking it in some random person's mouth. This is the reason Cee said she never wanted her own babies.

"Look at all these women," she'd say. "They pop out a kid and think motherhood adds a layer of bling to their fannies. I'm not ending up like them."

And it breaks my heart knowing she'll never have the choice. It's like everything I see now, everyone I look at, or walk by, or earwig on their conversations, adds another moment to the list of moments Cee will never experience.

I check my Insta post. The comments make me feel dizzy and nauseous.

Stop with the fake tears.

You weren't her friend. You used her cos you didn't have a life of your own.

Friends have their friends' backs.

I down my second shot. And a third.

"That's better." Tia cackles like a witch and I laugh with her.

"I'm back, baby," I yell at the mirror ball on the ceiling.

24

Kofi does a disappearing act somewhere around shot nine or ten. There was some kid in skinny jeans watching him and I think they went outside together for some 'fresh air.' It's good. I want Kofi to have a laugh and stop worrying about me; he has enough to worry about at home. And anyways, he hasn't said so, but I'm convinced he's still a virgin and it's about time we set that little record straight, so if I can sort him out with some half-decent geezer while we're here, it's one achievement more than I currently have under my belt.

Cheers to that.

The Abba tribute band kicks off with 'Mamma Mia'. After that, the songs all blur around the edges like someone sat on the mike, and I try dancing to 'Super Trouper' with Mum and Frankie the way Meryl Streep dances in the movie, but my legs are not cooperating, and I wish I'd eaten the box of Jaffa cakes I took along for the journey, but they're probably melted in the bottom of a carrier bag now. So, I ask some guy at the bar to buy me a packet of nuts instead, salted not dry-roasted.

"Cee can't eat dry roasted," I say. "She says they taste like vomit."

"Who's Cee?" He peers around me at our table. I follow his gaze, but I can't see her.

"She's gone," I say.

"She's not the only one." He wiggles his eyebrows at his mates who are so close now, which is surprising as I didn't notice them when I came over.

"What are you drinking?" one of his mates asks. He has spit in the corner of his mouth, and I can't take my eyes off it. "Hello?"

"I think she's had enough," says the first one. He hooks some change from his pocket and chucks it onto the bar. "Give us some nuts, love," he says to the barmaid.

"They ain't the kind of nuts she's after," says his mate. He reaches for my arm and pulls me closer to him as something inside me snaps awake.

"Let go of me." I wrench free of his grip, catching his mate's pint with my elbow as I turn.

"Fuck!" Beer spills over his wrist and onto his trainers. "My new trainers."

The others laugh but the guy who was buying my snack says, "Leave it, Daw. Let her go."

I don't wait around to thank him. All I know is, I need to get outside. Cee is gone, and all the vodka shots, and tequilas, and out-of-tune Abba songs in the world are not going to bring her back. I'm too hot; sweat clings to my hair extensions and I'm certain my armpits are wet. I can't breathe. My vision, blurred by tears, is narrowed to a few feet in front of me and if anyone steps in my way, I think, I'll mow them down.

Someone says, "What's up, babe?" as I stumble by, but I can't turn my head to look at her. If I turn, or stop, or breathe, I'll die of suffocation in this room with the ceiling dropping onto my head and the table too close together, and the sandal-sucking carpet.

People are staring. I catch my thigh against the corner of a table, and a man in a Homer Simpson T-shirt says, "Watch it!" as he grabs for the edge to stop the drinks from toppling.

A woman snatches her child from my path and gives me evils. Buggies are rolled aside, and backs are turned, but I don't care. Tears are soaking my cheeks and dripping into my top; a bruise is swelling on my leg and I don't remember where I left my bag, but I know I'll be able to breathe outside. Outside I'll catch my thoughts, wind them up like balls of different coloured knitting wool so I can tell them apart. Outside I'll cool down.

A huge family is gathering at the swing doors into the lobby, filling the space with excitement and laughter, like they own the fucking doors and no one else should want to use them, mums and dads and kids and bloody grandparents. I charge straight at them. My need is greater than theirs, because if I don't get through those doors I'll die, and they'll have to pick up the broken fragments of my heart and mind and soul, and that'll ruin their holiday more than not getting a table near the dance floor.

Maybe my imminent death is scrawled across my forehead because panic trips across their faces and kick-starts them into moving away from the entrance to let me through, and if I wasn't so desperate to get outside and breathe real air, I'd have laughed out loud. Their comments of "What the hell?" and, "She's pissed," follow me out into the evening which is still fuzzy-warm and heavy with the last layer of sunshine. I keep running.

I don't know where I'm going. Standing tall on the other side of the clubhouse is the big wheel and the rollercoaster, the screams and yelling and laughter a dead giveaway that it's even busier there than it is inside the ballroom. I don't want to see people so I veer away from the lights and sirens and jingles, past the crazy-golf course where families with kids are still tallying up their scores, past the tennis courts and the closed go-kart circuit, past the sheds where the four-seat canopy bikes are stored, following the path like it's the yellow brick road and I mustn't leave it till I reach the Emerald City.

The Emerald City appears as a mirage of the outdoor swimming pool. There's no one swimming; I guess alcohol and this kind of exercise don't really mix. Somehow, I scale the low fence, cut through a gap in the hedge protecting the sun loungers and palm trees in huge terracotta pots, past the giant stripy deckchair and the plastic Nessie, and head to the large pool where the water is bluest. Only then, when I stand at the edge of the deep end and stare into the easy ripples, do I breathe.

In, out, swallow, blink back the tears, wring my fingers which have a life of their own as my brain is no longer in control. I bend over and tug off my heels. The soles of my feet are screaming at me for having pushed them too hard in totally impractical footwear. My heart hurts. It's such an effort to breathe when there's a gaping Cee-size wound in my chest. I sink to my knees at the poolside.

I can't live without her. I don't want to live without her smile, and her crazy-adventure ideas, and her frustration at the life she'd been given, because they were the qualities that made her so adorable. She was vulnerable. She was beautiful.

And it hurts to think of her in past tense. Where has the rest of her life gone? There's a path that was solely hers to be followed, to be filled along the way with love, and jobs, and holidays, and babies; where's that dream now? I can't believe it just vanishes. I can't.

Sitting on the side of the pool, I rest my head on my knees, folding the hurt inside of me so it can't escape. It's what I deserve: this pain, these tears. I deserve to cry myself into a puddle that slips into the cool blue deep end, and down the plug hole into the drains, and out to sea, where the only reminder I was ever here will be my dress, and my stupid gold sandals that I can't even walk in. But even my tears won't behave. Within minutes I'm reduced to choking sobs that make me cough, and splutter, and I open my eyes to check no one can hear, because even in my grief I'm aware someone might be watching and thinking, *Jesus, she's a mess.* Not if they can't see me though.

I squint through my tears. The pool area is secluded. The trees are tall; they muffle the sounds of the fairground attractions, the screams from the rides, and the rumble of cars on tracks, the hooter signalling the start of the Dodgems and the tinny tunes of the carousel, but if someone was to peer closely through the foliage, they'd still see the drunk girl in the sparkly dress crouching by the side of the pool.

I need to get in. A quick glance all around to check I'm alone, and I whip my dress over my head and slide into the water. It's colder than it looks. This end of the pool is in shadow with the sun lower in the sky, the water dark and mysterious, and within minutes my skin is bobbled and I'm shivering. The combination of cold water and alcohol numbs my brain, and clinging to the side, I inch along till my feet touch the floor and my chin rests on the surface, and turn to face the cool blue, embracing the emptiness I've been waiting for.

It's peaceful. The only interruptions to the calm are my shivers, but even they cease as my flesh acclimatises to the water temperature, and new random disjointed thoughts start to sneak back in. I think of the *Titanic* movie, of how Jack stays in the icy water at the end while Rose is blue-lipped and shivering on the wooden door, and I still wish he'd climbed on too, and Celine Dion sings 'My Heart Will Go On' but I can't quite hear the words right now.

The last film I saw at the cinema was *A Star is Born,* and the people in the audience were sobbing; there's always people dying, and crying, but where are my tears when I want them? If I was at home, I'd get Mac to put CBeebies on the telly for Jonah so he could see the colours, and there'll be no tears on CBeebies—you can't show kids sad stuff because they'll have nightmares. And I don't know what autoimmune system means. I think we learned about it in school one time, like Mussolini, and figureheads, and how to make an omelette, but I don't remember, and it's scary all the things I don't remember already, because it means I'm losing memories all over the place, and one day Cee will be gone forever.

I try to concentrate on the last thing we did together. We went to a farm and saw baby lambs; the farmer was using sign language to tell us about how they feed, and Jonah was bleeding. I'm confused. Where were the lambs? Jonah wasn't bleeding, he was dipping his fingers in red paint. A finger painting. Mr Tumble said . . . what did he say? I'm rubbish at sign language.

I hear a tapping sound close by and I realise it's my teeth chattering. I move my arms a fraction, and the cold bites into newly exposed flesh. One movement leads to another, like a contagious disease, all my reflexes jumping and bolting, but I don't have the energy to climb out, because outside is worse than this. But there are other sounds. Voices. I open my eyes and see only water, darker now, with silver ripples on the surface which make me think of the woods at night and my bear-wolf. She'd make me warm again. I need to find her.

"Don't just stand there."

The words slice through my numb brain cells. The voice is familiar, and suddenly I know Cee has come back for me.

"Cee," I say, but my throat is clogged up with frozen tears, the way the plughole in the bathroom sink gets blocked with Mum's hair.

"Not a fucking one of you thought to get her out."

"We didn't know what to do."

"We were waiting for security."

"Fuck security! You want her locked up in a fucking loony bin?"

Soft footsteps by the side of the pool, and another sound: a zip, clothes dropping to the floor, a splash. And suddenly there are arms around me, warm and bony, and whispers, "Okay, baby girl. It'll all be okay. We'll just get you out of here."

A new voice outside of us: "What's going on? Is she okay?"

"Lizzie's got her."

"I'll get some towels." Panic-footsteps running away.

Mum scoops me into her arms and I cling to her neck, burying my face in her shampoo and perfume and cigarette smell as she swims clumsily along the side, one hand gripping the edge until we reach the steps, and there are other hands waiting to help us out.

The back of my head hits the ground as I spill out of the pool, but Mum is kneeling over me, hair dripping onto my face. She smooths water from my cheeks.

"Summer, don't worry, baby. We'll get you out of here." She turns away. "Don't just stand there. One of you get a towel or something."

"Kofi's gone to get one."

"Well stand closer so no one can see."

There's panic in her voice that I can remember from another occasion, another time, another universe, when Cee's lips were blue, and I was begging her to wake up.

A hand cradles my head, and she's wiping my face with something, a jacket or a pair of shorts, and she murmurs, "Stay awake, Summer. I'll make it better, sweetheart, I promise."

25

And for eight days, eighteen hours and forty-nine minutes, she does.

Snotty and feverish for the first couple of days after we come home, I hibernate under a duvet while the rest of the world swelters in twenty-five degrees, staring at the telly without seeing, and dreading the dark which is when death appears in a floor-length black coat and attempts to drag me through the mattress and down into the underworld. It's obviously where I deserve to be. I don't recall much of what happened at Butlin's, at least that's what I tell Mum.

She wears her mum-hat gracefully, only pinning it back for the exercise bike and to stop Jonah tugging on it, because that boy has got some grip. We slip into a kind of routine where I feed Jonah his morning bottle while she's in the shower, and then we eat cereal in the living room with the patio doors open, and Jonah in his vibrating baby seat in front of the telly so he can follow the light, and colours, and movement. His little legs kick like crazy whenever he sees *In the Night Garden* and we discover, by the way he flaps, that his favourite song video is George Ezra's *Pretty Shining People.*

In the afternoons she prepares a salad and pasta, or kebabs, or barbecue chicken, for dinner. When she pushes hers around the plate and pretends to eat, I pretend I don't notice, because it would burst the bubble that we've created around us and hurtle me kicking and screaming back to teenage reality in all its horrific glory, and minus my best friend. Mac smiles because she's not mentioned the Ovary for days, and he's probably thinking the whole lantern ceremony thing is forgotten.

Notes still plop on to the doormat, and we spread them out across the kitchen counter and laugh at them.

"You'd think the fat bitch would be bored by now," Mum says.

When she isn't looking, I sneak them down to my bedroom and tuck them away with the others.

Gran comes round in the afternoons with some end-of-line stock for us to root through, or magazines, or tins of mushroom soup and corned beef; they're like little peace offerings handed over at the threshold to appease the daughter and granddaughter goddesses and make the visit tick over like one of those antique clocks where you can see the cogs turning. God knows what she thinks will happen if she turns up empty-handed. We don't mention the pool incident.

I wonder if Mum has told Gran in a hushed telephone conversation while I'm asleep, because she strokes my arm whenever she sees me, and asks how the bridesmaid plans are going, and if I've sorted my wedding makeup, and did I get so drunk on the weekend I can't remember what happened?

I say, "Fine, Gran, everything's going fine."

I've had one message from Tia since the hen weekend which I ignored, and my final dress fitting is in two weeks' time.

The days pass by like a Netflix series waiting for the next

cliff-hanger. And it appears on day eight in the shape of Danielle. She arrives as she always does, juggling the buggy and way too many bags for a single visit, talking about twenty things at once and eyes all over the place so she doesn't miss anything. She's brought a fresh jar of butterscotch flavoured coffee granules and a tub of sweeteners.

Since baby Milla arrived, Danielle has metamorphosed from a whale to an eel, all slippery and skinny, with greenish veins, and ivory bones, and transparent skin. She slithers around the house like a duck in mud, never seeming to do anything with the babies and yet succeeding in doing everything they need in order to exist.

Normally they spend their time gossiping about who's shagging who, and whose life is nothing like their Instagram account because they know full well, she don't look like that without makeup, and he was spotted in the Inn with an eighteen-year-old, and on and on. But this time she deposits the kids in front of the telly, chucks an, "Alright, Summer?" my way, and they scuttle into the kitchen, lean against the counter, the two of them, whispering.

Franco watches me. I poke my tongue out at him and he pokes his tongue out too. It's a strange experience. With Jonah I can adopt a sing-song voice and repeat myself at least three times without feeling like a twat, but Franco, although not yet a child capable of holding a full-blown conversation, has progressed beyond the innocent joy of listening to a constant babble of nonsense words, and watches me with a frown scrunching the smooth dark skin between his eyebrows like he's trying to work out what kind of mother I am. It scares me so much that we sit in the living room in awkward silence.

I glance away first. I've no idea how old Franco is but I'm sure he can talk. I flick through channels with the remote and find *Mr Tumble*. Still, he stares at me like I'm an alien with his eyes that are the same colour as Kofi's. I make a mental note to tell Mac about *Mr Tumble*; we should buy DVDs for when Jonah is older.

"Hide me." Franco is leaning heavily against my knees. He doesn't smile. "Hide me," he repeats.

"I can't hide you," I say quickly, glancing around the room; I have no idea where I'd put him.

"Hide me," he says again, taking my hand and pushing it up to my face.

"He wants you to close your eyes so he can hide." Danielle translates from the doorway and disappears again before I can speak.

I cover my eyes leaving a crack between fingers so I can still follow Franco. Trusting me completely, he heads straight for the box of baby toys in the corner of the room, selects Jonah's butterfly rattle and tucks it into Milla's baby bag. Then the little creep stands in the middle of the room waiting for me.

I remove my hands. "You're not hiding," I say.

"Hide you," he says.

"I'm not hiding. I'm too big." This is a silly game and he's not even playing properly.

"Hide you." He takes my hand and pulls. He's persistent.

"Okay." I stand. "Close your eyes."

He kneels on the floor and rests his face on the sofa cushion. Holding my breath, like he might hear it, I tiptoe across the carpet to Milla's bag and slip the rattle out. It's Jonah's. They're not taking it home. But, glancing at Franco's dark exposed neck where he's bent over the sofa, he looks so vulnerable and tiny, and it suddenly pings in my brain like a microwave, that he's done what I used to do when I was a little girl. If my mum left a pendant or a string of coordinated beads hanging on the corner of the bathroom mirror, or the bedroom door handle, I'd move the toilet step, climb up and take them.

At Gran's, when she was busy cooking dinner and Grandad was polishing a speck of dust off his shiny car, I'd sneak into their bedroom and take a jewel from Gran's treasure chest. They were the best because Gran had real jewels.

I remember when one of Mum's boyfriends left us, and Mum forgot to eat. She forgot she had a daughter who needed to eat too, and Gran had arrived with a suitcase full of clothes smelling of Grandad, and said the house needed de-cluttering. "Tidy rooms, tidy minds."

The house was rearranged, new furniture ordered for the living room, and Grandad paid decorators to paint the walls.

"Clean start," Gran said. Mum wanted red walls. "Maybe something a little less dangerous," suggested Gran, so they settled for magnolia because Mum had lost interest.

My room had to be tidied too, including under the bed. Gran's pink lipstick had worn away on the inside and stuck to her teeth and only the outline remained. If she knew, she'd have fetched her handbag and topped it up, but I didn't tell her. Gran's hand came out from under the bed with a fistful of beads. She showed them to me as if I might not have seen them before.

"Where did these come from?" Some of Gran's beads were there, the shiniest and the prettiest, but most of them were Mum's.

"I found them," I said in a small voice.

Gran rolled them around in the palm of her hand with one finger. I was certain she recognised her own, because she picked up one large diamond teardrop and rolled it back and forth in the light from the window.

"Pretty, aren't they?" she said finally. "They shouldn't be under the bed gathering dust." She tucked them into my jewellery box. "There, we can forget about them now, lovey."

Any second now, Franco would turn around and accuse me of not hiding. I scan the windowsills, the shelves of the wall unit, the shelf under the coffee table for something to give him. And then I spot the crystals on the top shelf beside a porcelain fairy; they were from the 'crystals-for-every-mood' phase which lasted about three and a half days. I pick up a shiny brown one sparkly with gold flecks; she won't miss it. She probably doesn't even remember they're there. Crossing the room, I slip the crystal into the pocket of Franco's joggers and stand back, proud of myself.

"I'm done," I say.

He doesn't glance at me. He takes the crystal from his pocket and stares at it in the palm of his hand, and my heart is fluttering with the desperate hope that he likes it.

And that's when I hear them in the kitchen.

"If they'd found her, they'd have had her straight into a loony bin."

"That's not what you want, Liz, especially after what happened, you know."

I picture their raised eyebrows, their pinched mouths, and their nods in my direction. I crouch down.

"It's a crystal," I say to Franco. My voice is shaky, and I don't know why. "It's a special crystal for a special boy, okay. Can you say crystal?"

He looks at me but doesn't speak.

"You need to keep it somewhere safe, like . . ." I feel around for his toys. He has a Buzz Lightyear, a few small cars, and a Mr Potato Head. "Here," I say, opening the flap on the back of the potato's head. "Put your crystal in here so you can take it home."

Franco does as he's told, his bottom lip rolled out in concentration. Flap closed; I place the toy back in the bag. I just hope he'll remember it when he gets home.

"Do you want an ice cream?"

He puts his warm hand in mine in response. Leading him to the kitchen, I realise their voices have dropped again to whispers, and as we reach the doorway, Mum is dropping a mobile phone into a box of cornflakes.

"Summer," she says when she notices me. The box is placed at the back of the top cupboard above the kettle. "I thought you were keeping an eye on the kids."

"We want ice cream," I say.

"Oh, baby, you want ice cream?" Danielle scoops up her son and buries her face in the crook of his neck, but I've seen her flushed cheeks.

"What shall we give him, Dan?" asks Mum, making a big show of crouching in front of the freezer and scraping ice crystals off a box of lollies. "I've got these." She holds up a strawberry lolly. "Or we've got vanilla ice cream but no cones. What will he eat?" She's talking so I can't ask questions.

It's okay. I know where she put the phone.

I take Franco to the park . . . at least, that's what I tell them. I want him to meet my bear-wolf. I've never wanted anyone else to see her, but after watching Franco with the crystal, it feels as though I can see right inside his skull. Even his silence no longer resembles demon-baby. He only wants attention.

Holding his hand as we walk along, I wonder if this is how Cee felt when she was walking with Demi, or Drew. Grown-up. Responsible. His podgy little hand in mine feels like cradling a baby creature that's wandered away from its mother. I should never let him go until I know that he is safe. But more than that, his skin is almost the same shade as Ritchie's—Franco's dad being mixed-race—so I feel like he is our baby, mine and Ritchie's. He's our baby, and I'm introducing him to the bear-wolf so that he never has to feel lonely.

When we reach the hollow, she is sleepy and slow, her nose nudging my arm away so that she can see Franco.

"This is Franco," I tell her. "He's like me."

She seems to accept that because she lays on her side so that he can stroke her whiskers and the hair on the top of her head, and his hand rubs her fur back and forth, and I realise it's the first time I've ever seen him smile.

"We should've brought your crystal," I tell him. "You see, these are mine." I show him the trinkets and beads and shiny belts that I've accumulated over time, like a magpie stealing other birds' glitter.

Franco still doesn't speak, but he reaches into his other pocket and pulls out a tiny transparent bag which he tosses onto my lap. My heart freezes in my chest and then speeds up again as though someone has fast-forwarded us with an invisible remote. I hold the bag up in front of my face. It's dark in here, but I need to be sure that these are what I think they are. Pills.

He is still stroking the bear-wolf who is purring gently like she is snoring. "Franco, where did you get these?" I ask.

But he doesn't answer.

26

The phone is locked. It's an old Nokia, pay-as-you-go probably, a basic handset must've only cost twenty quid. I try 1-2-3-4; it doesn't work. I try the year Mum was born, and it unlocks. She obviously knows nothing about password security.

There are five unread text messages from someone called Staffie. Ugh! By sliding on the notification, I can read the last text without physically opening the message.

What about a feather boa? Next time. And wear the stockings.

I don't know which one of them the phone belongs to, but I do know it's not normal to keep a phone inside a Cornflakes box. I set it back down exactly how I found it and replace the box in the cupboard next to the Weetabix. I hope Mac wants Cornflakes for breakfast at the weekend because I won't offer to make it for him.

"I want a Pandora necklace," I say.

"And I want to be the bloody queen." She's on the balcony practising her sexy smoke-ring technique. I imagine her in a club with Danielle, sucking on a lollipop and offering it to the first guy who gives her the eye. I've seen Tia do it, rolling it around on her tongue, and licking her lips before shoving it in a guy's mouth, but it's normally someone she knows, or the mate of someone she knows, and it gets a laugh because it isn't deep. But this, this is serious stuff. The way they dress, the way they drink and huddle together over their little private phone, it's calculated; they know what they're doing.

"The others are all getting one for the wedding."

"Summer I'm not made of money."

She has new Havaianas flip-flops on her feet, denim shorts with a diamante buckled belt, a new hairband holding back the mane, and every time she goes out, she wears a new outfit. Jonah is laying in his teddy bear gym. His romper is cute: grey and white stripes with a raised zebra motif on the front to match the soft toy beside him, and the duvet in the Moses basket. We coordinate. We can't be seen to be wearing mismatched outfits, because that will spoil the obligatory photos of our perfect life on our perfect Instagram accounts.

"So, you want me to look ridiculous," I say. I don't care about the necklace; I made it up. I don't even know what accessories they're wearing, and I've not spoken to them since Butlin's.

"No one will even bloody notice." She flicks her cigarette over the balcony somewhere in the direction of the heap of fag ends in the corner of the bottom yard, and steps back into the living room, hazy in the glow of daylight.

She'd notice. She'd be the first to comment that someone's mother couldn't put their hand in their pocket and fork out for a decent necklace to complement the dress.

"You'd notice."

"Summer, what's this all about?" She checks her phone, slips it back into the rear pocket of her shorts. She's calculating the precise time to get the bike out: bike, shower, fake tan, sling some sausages in the oven before Mac gets home. A conversation about a Pandora necklace isn't on the schedule and doesn't warrant the time she's already allocated to it.

"It's about me fitting in. Isn't that what you've always wanted? Didn't you want me to tell stories in assembly about my ski instructor, and my new five hundred quid watch, and my stash of Apple products? That's impressive, isn't it? Who needs an education when you've got money?"

"You do fit in, Summer. What the hell you on about?" She's unzipping her shorts; it must be time for the bike to come out.

Jonah's arms flap and he bats a furry sheep above his head. He's due a feed any time now but she wouldn't know that.

"I can't even get my makeup done with the rest of them. What's the point of me even being bridesmaid? They'll all look the same, and there'll be me at the back looking like I do on a Saturday night."

"Summer," her voice has softened but only because she wants me to shut up. "You always look stunning."

It's not about the necklace. It's not about me fitting in. I can't put my finger on what it is about, but her eyes don't meet mine, they don't settle on Jonah, they don't even register the telly, or the sunshine, or the fly bashing its head against the window. She's not here. Not really. She's anywhere else but here, probably propping up a bar with Danielle.

That's what I see when I throw my phone across the room and watch it bounce off the windowsill.

"What?" She whirls around to figure out what happened. "Did you just throw your phone?"

"I want a necklace." My face is hot, and tears are squeezing out of the corners of my eyes. If my phone is smashed, I might lose my photos of Cee, and our messages, and I don't know what I'll do if I can't see her beautiful face again. Why can't she just get me a necklace?

"I want a necklace," I repeat.

She stands with her hands on her hips, her face pale, her chest rising dramatically as she breathes, the bones protruding above her vest. "Pick up your phone, Summer. Don't think I'm buying you another new one."

She might've been telling five-year-old me to finish my breakfast, or tidy my room, or teenage me to get out of bed and get ready for school. Her voice is shrill with the fear and certainty of losing the battle.

Instinctively my body reacts the way it always has done. "No!" I yell like a toddler, snatching at the cushion and burying my face in it. "I don't care if it's broken. I don't care if you won't buy me a new one."

"Go without then."

I sense rather than see her leave the room and I move on to the next tactic: the red danger button. "Fine!" I snap. "I'll tell Gran you won't buy me a necklace. I'll tell her you're going out every night with Danielle, and I'll tell her about—"

"Okay, okay." She's back in the room. Her eyes almost disappear she rolls them so far into the back of her head, and her mouth is a button. "I'll get you a fucking necklace, just stop your bloody whining and pick up your phone." She glances at Jonah as if he might toss in a comment about her

181

parenting skills, but he's still engrossed in the fluffy sheep floating above his head.

It works every time. Why isn't she stronger? I feel sorry for Jonah because he'll get everything he wants too.

Mum wasn't searching for a father for me, at least that's what she told Gran. Her boyfriends spoke to me in silly voices, tried too hard to make me smile. "See," they said to her, "you have to be on the same wavelength is all."

Joe wasn't like the others. He talked in his real voice. Smiled with his eyes. Joe spent as much time with me as he did with her.

When we went to the park or to the beach, he bought me ice cream and a plastic bucket and spade, and we built sandcastles with turrets and a moat that we filled with foamy seawater carried across the sand in my bucket. We made shell-windows and feather-flags and hunted for teeny-tiny crabs to guard the moat. And if anyone came near my castle he'd say, "Watch out, mate."

Joe bought me a stripy cardigan that I wore all the time, even to bed, even when Mum said, "Christ, Summer, it needs a bloody wash, or they'll smell you coming."

On my birthday he arrived with a pink shiny scooter. "Special scooter for a special little lady," he said.

At the park he carried the scooter up the hill with one hand. I kept my eyes on my sandaled feet, and my arms in my new cardigan, even though they itched and my face sweated, because I had to run to keep up with him.

He held the scooter while I climbed aboard, set me off

down the slope and ran after me to make sure I didn't fall, because Mummy wouldn't be happy if I was hurt, and she had to patch me up. So many times, I couldn't count, way more times than ten, I rode down the hill until we were both out of breath and thirsty and happy. Mum waited at the bottom where the grass was flat, and she could see the other mothers with their children in the play area. She lay on the grass with her knees bent and her top pulled low, sunglasses protecting her eyes and the grass tickling her toes.

When we stopped for a drink of water, she said, "Why don't you stay with me?" She said this to Joe. She was lonely.

"Will you be okay, Summer?" he asked, eyes squinting against the sun, elbows resting on his knees.

I nodded. I dragged my heavy scooter up the steep hill, alone, with slow feet that tried to trip me up, and a voice inside my head telling me if I fell and cut my knees, it was nothing less than I deserved. I saw the woods all dark and silent, filled with hiding places for creatures, and I wished Joe had never bought the scooter.

From the bottom of the hill, sitting on the grass beside Mummy he waved at me, shielding his eyes from the sun with his other hand. I think he might've called out, but the words were blown away by the breeze that tickled the leaves. On the field some big boys were playing football, and past them some men dressed in white trousers were playing cricket. There were children on the swings, and the roundabout, and the climbing frame. People were walking dogs.

On my own at the top of the hill, I felt like the man in the moon. I wondered how it would feel to spread my arms and fly down to the bottom, or simply to hang above the sky, floating, seeing everything that was going on without anyone realising I was watching.

Joe waved again. He stood, and Mummy reached out a hand to touch his leg; he glanced down at her before turning back to watch me.

He knew what I was going to do but he was split in two, and the half that belonged to my mum was more important because they had sleepovers.

I let go of the scooter and watched it rattle and tumble all the way to the bottom of the hill.

Mac is watching us from the top of a hill. One eye on Mum and the other on Jonah, I barely enter his peripheral vision and my stomach twists because no amount of bonding will ever make me his little girl; I'm a teenager on a swing huddled over her phone messaging a boy or checking out her Instagram feed. Invisible. Even the notes pushed through the letterbox fail to raise an eyebrow, like he has bigger things going on, priorities.

And they bicker all the time. "I fancy a roast," Mac announces one Sunday morning when she's buried her eyes in hollows above her cheekbones, and her hair clings to last night's cigarettes.

"I'm not cooking a roast," she says. "I've got better things to do with my time."

Yeah, like playing Candy Crush.

"I'll cook the bloody roast," Mac says.

"There's no veg in the freezer."

"Oh yes because that's where veg grows these days."

Stupid arguments, over stupid inconsequential subjects. I begin to wonder which one of us is the adult.

The impending lantern ceremony sits like a hippo in the corner of the room, while we all tiptoe around it pretending it isn't there. Mum sneering at it sideways because she thinks she's won; she thinks she can make me go. Mac is oblivious to the upcoming event because he thinks it's a done deal I'm not going. I develop stomach cramps, and blurry headaches, and a heart rate that'd challenge that geezer who won gold medal at the Olympics, Mo whatever-his-name-is. I try to work out how I can have my own ceremony, set off my own lantern somewhere quiet, just me and Cee.

And then Mum goes and ruins everything.

27

Jonah has a hospital appointment: tests on his heart and lungs, because sometimes children with Down's syndrome develop problems and it's best if they catch them early. Mac comes back with the baby and McDonald's; Mum has gone to Gran's shop because she doesn't quite have enough clothes in her wardrobes. She says anyway. I'm re-watching *Gossip Girl*. I can't be bothered to do anything else. I have no energy, my brain has given up on me, consumed by images of Chinese bloody lanterns and notes written in black felt tip.

My thoughts keep returning to school. If I sit my exams next year, I could go to college and do a beauty course, get my own salon one day and maybe learn how to do lip fillers and microdermabrasion. But at the thought of reading a book, or writing an essay, or multiplying fractions, my brain cells panic and a migraine scrubs away at the inside of my skull.

The notes though—I can read them okay. I can read them with my eyes closed. Without taking them out of my jewellery box and unfolding them I could recite each one, word for miserable word.

Mac's in and out, making phone calls and scratching his balls. He said they have to wait for the results but nothing major had flagged up, whatever that means. When he isn't looking, I kiss Jonah's forehead, a silent apology for leaving him, and go downstairs to my room to watch telly. I haven't been out of the house for days. I haven't washed, I haven't dressed, I've not replied to any messages, most of which have been from Kofi. The girls have been out for Frankie's birthday, photos of them pissed and posing behind shiny pink balloons, plastered all over Facebook and they didn't even ask if I wanted to go.

I might've fallen asleep halfway through season one on my phone, because when I wake up Mum's in the shower. The front door opens and Mac's keys jangle onto the hook in the hallway; I didn't hear either of them come in or go out. Cupboards open and close in the kitchen, a ring pull pops, the smell of frying minced meat wafts downstairs and makes me gag. Whatever he's cooking, I don't want it.

Rolling onto my side I stare out of the window at the bottom yard. Crap has blown down from the upstairs garden and collected in soggy mounds along the bottom of the shed. It's a mess. My dressing table needs cleaning: eyelashes like fringes are collecting dust under the mirror, scrunched up dirty makeup wipes are everywhere, the surface is more foundation smudges than clean space. My bedding needs washing too, but I'm clinging to the smell of Cee. I know once it's washed it'll be the last remaining traces of her lost forever.

I hear Mum thump upstairs; for a skinny lady she carries a lot of baggage on her shoulders. I hear the murmur of voices, Mac laughing, probably on his phone.

And then the world ends. The scream is horrible. My heart thumps madly, convinced that something has happened to

Jonah. I throw back my duvet and run up the stairs to the living room.

Mac reaches the living room one step ahead of me. She's standing beside the Moses basket, her hand clamped over her mouth, her face ghastly white, and I think Jonah must've been kidnapped while we've all been in our other worlds.

"What? What is it?" Mac's voice is tight with panic. He stops so abruptly I almost head-butt his back. "Lizzie, what?" He takes a step closer.

"Don't you come near me!" she screeches. "Don't you come anywhere near me or my son!" She's standing in front of the Moses basket, hands spread wide protectively, chest heaving, legs shaking, and I can't figure out why her words sound all wrong.

"What the fuck are you talking about?" Mac crosses the room in two steps, grabs her shoulders, and moves her aside. He bends over the basket and pulls back the blanket. His face changes, I watch it in slow motion. "Hello there, beautiful boy," he says in his Jonah-voice. Still bent, he glances up at her, mouths, "What's wrong?" and shrugs.

The telly is off, and Adele is singing on the radio. Everything is back to normal. But she doesn't answer. Instead, she lunges at Mac with such force, he crashes backwards into the wall, arms spread to catch his balance as she springs backwards.

"What's wrong?" she screams. "What's wrong? Look what you've done to him." She punches Mac's chest, hands like hammers beating a gong. I hear the thuds. I hear them, but I don't understand them.

"Stop!" Mac tries to catch her wrists but only succeeds in veering her blows to his neck. He groans out loud. "Lizzie! Stop!"

But she's crying and screaming at the same time. "You bastard! You absolute bloody bastard!"

I've seen fights in school. Bundles. Boys with their shirts ripped out of their school trousers, blazers hanging off shoulders and school bags spilling science textbooks over the playground. Children would crowd around chanting, jeering them on, rooting for the one who appears to be winning or the one they're most scared of, or the one they fancy the most. They'd kick each other's legs and hold onto arms and belts and anything else they can grab hold of, pink-cheeked and occasionally even crying. They aren't real fights, I realise now.

This is real and scary. I can't breathe and I can't think. She's punching, and slapping, and sobbing while Mac, on the floor, crosses his arms in self-defence, and I know that if she pushes him too far and he snaps, one punch will break her jaw or worse. I should call someone, but my arms are glued to my side.

Somehow, Mac manages to gain his balance, drag himself upright, and pin her arms behind her back. "Stop for one fucking second," he says, panting.

"You smoked that shit near him," she shouts, already hoarse.

"I what? No! No, I haven't smoked anywhere—"

"Look at him! Look at him!" she struggles to free her arms, kicks out against his shins.

"What?" Mac releases his grip for a second to peer down at Jonah and she lashes out, catches the side of his face with her nails. He tries to avoid landing on the baby and falls instead onto the dining table. A chair gives way beneath him and he crashes to the floor, splintered wood buckling beneath his weight.

But she doesn't stop. She's like a crazy woman, black hair

matted across her face, skinny arms punching and slapping at random. "You've burnt him," she cries between sobs. "You've fucking burnt him, and they'll take him away."

I see Mac raise his knees to his chest. I see her lurch backwards, smothered with hair, and land on her back on the Gryffindor rug in the living room. I hear the crack of her head against the leg of the coffee table. A mug careens onto the floor spilling waves of muddy coffee onto the carpet. She doesn't move.

In the pause, Mac grips the Moses basket, peers again at Jonah. I wait for whatever injury she's accusing him of to register in his face, in some reaction. He doesn't speak. Blood trickles down his cheek and onto his football shirt, red spots oozing beneath his eye.

"I-did-not-do-that," he says finally. He strokes Jonah's face and I wait for the baby to scream with pain, but there's no sound from him.

The way Mac looks at her is awful. His eyes are narrow, cruel. They are not the eyes of someone in love.

Raising one hand to his face, he pulls away bloody fingers. "I love the way you just accuse me," he says, his voice low and cold. "You stupid bitch. Whatever you think I've done, I love my son, and *that* is not a burn." He passes me on his way to the kitchen. I don't have time to move or to hide but I'm invisible anyway. He returns a few seconds later, chest heaving with the effort of controlling his temper. "You smoke too, remember? Maybe I should be accusing you of hurting him."

She clambers up from the floor and follows him, still screaming, like she hasn't heard a word he said. "You're the one who smokes that shit!"

"I'm the one who loves him!"

It's funny how your body can move of its own accord even when you think you're incapable of action. I cross the room to my baby brother in his Moses basket. His eyes are wide open, arms and legs wriggling freely where the blanket has been loosened.

It's several seconds before I notice the red mark in the centre of his forehead like a Bindi worn by Hindu women. A perfect red mark. Like a dot of paint so close to his hairline it's almost hidden. Jonah smiles up at me, shows me his pink gums, oblivious to the war raging on in the kitchen. I kissed him before I went downstairs. I squeeze my eyes closed and try to picture his perfect face. Was the mark there? Has it always been there?

I pick him up and take him downstairs to my messy, silent room so Cee and I can take care of him.

28

"You need to get over here and see what your son has done." She's upstairs but she might as well be in the room with us, I can hear her so clearly.

Mac has gone out. I heard him race down the stairs, empty drawers, and yank clothes from hangers, his sports bag banging against the door frame as he headed back up. The door slammed. The house shook. He threatened to take the baby to his parents' house but must've changed his mind when she threatened to tell the police he was kidnapping him.

I study the red dot on Jonah's head. It isn't livid, or sore, or scabby, and when I touch it lightly with my finger, he smiles at me, curls his fat fingers around mine, drags my hand towards his mouth. Two thoughts bounce around inside my head. I've seen a cigarette burn. Kofi has a row of them like shiny pearly buttons on the inside of his arm—the bastard counted one more chicken drumstick on his stepson's plate than his own and decided to dish out a painful little reminder, one scar for each piece of meat. This doesn't look like the burns on Kofi's arm. It isn't inflamed and it doesn't look fresh either, like charred skin, the thought of which makes me feel sick. And the baby isn't crying. Surely a cigarette burn would be torture, and he'd be screaming his head off? We'd have heard it when it happened. Wouldn't we?

Also, the Mac I've seen who sets Jonah down so gently on the changing mat in the evenings and uses his baby-voice when he's changing a nappy, or feeding him a bottle, isn't a man capable of scarring his own son. And for what purpose? Why would he do that to an innocent baby? To get at her for going out?

I don't buy it. Maybe it's some kind of rash. Why didn't she call the NHS Helpline or something instead of screaming at Mac?

"Your bastard son has hurt my baby, that's what's going on."

The kettle is filled and switched on to boil. Cupboard doors bounce and jangle. Footsteps pace from the kitchen to the patio doors: a nicotine fix while she waits for caffeine. I wait for her to come down and find us, examine the mark on Jonah's forehead, call the doctor or the health visitor, or someone who will know what to do. But she stays upstairs.

"It's okay, baby," I whisper, my lips close to his cheek. "I'm here."

"This is so bizarre," Cee says from the end of the bed.

"What is?"

"You and a baby. It's not something I ever imagined you doing, like, you were always the one with the perfect makeup and the longest hair extensions. I was the one who had to sneak the Ovary's heels out in an Asda bag, and find soggy biscuits squashed inside my pockets." She smiles, head tilted. "It suits you."

"He's just so . . . helpless," I say. "And he's not like other children."

"Are you sure he isn't yours?" She laughs but not so loudly to be heard upstairs.

"I wish he was. I'd bring him up to be nice to girls."

"No chance, Summer. It's in their genes to be fuck-boys."

"Not my boy."

She stretches out onto her stomach and strokes Jonah's fine wispy hair. "What makes you think he'll be different?"

"Because he's special."

"We're all special, only we're too scared to show it."

"You weren't, Cee. You weren't scared of anything."

She closes her eyes and remains so still I begin to wonder if she's fallen asleep. "I *was* scared," she says eventually. "I was scared because the road never seemed long enough, and I knew I had to jump in every hole, and smell every daisy, before I reached the end."

Her words draw more tears from my eyes. She must've known hers was to be a short life. Like a star, she had her moment to shine, and in a blink, it was over. It's so unfair. Why did she have a heart condition? Why didn't it have more heartbeats left to give her? Why couldn't a cruel person die in her place, a murderer or a rapist, someone rotting in a prison cell because they're too evil to be allowed back into the world? There are people like that. Why do they deserve long lives?

The doorbell rings. I stare hard at the door waiting for Mac's voice to reach us down here, my heart fluttering like a million butterflies. Maybe she'll listen if he comes back and explains he can't possibly have hurt Jonah. She does listen sometimes. When she wants to.

But it's the skinny grandparents. Their voices are hushed like they don't want the neighbours to hear, like they have no idea how thin these walls are. She doesn't care though; she's still ranting, her voice growing hoarser the more she goes on.

There's a quick rap on my door before it opens. I glance at Cee, but she's already gone.

"How are we doing, Summer?" It's David. He leans on the door handle, speaking at me but staring at Jonah, searching for the problem. "Shall we bring the baby upstairs so Marian can look him over?" He always speaks so precisely, his lips hardly moving like his words might evaporate before he gets his point across, should he open his mouth too wide.

I pick Jonah up, my hands around his chest, skinny legs dangling, and David quickly steps forward to place a hand on the back of his head.

"Careful now," he says.

"I've got him," I say. I would've let David carry him, but not now.

In the living room, Marian takes him without waiting for me to hand him over. She settles his head on her left arm, her zombie eyes scanning the red mark on his forehead. "That looks like a strawberry naevus to me," she says. David stands by her side.

"It wasn't there earlier." Mum stands by the patio doors, one foot inside and one outside, cigarette between her fingers. She doesn't come any closer.

"They do just appear sometimes," Marian explains. "They're not always born with them. Mac had one on his thigh. Did Jonah not have a hospital appointment this morning?"

"Yes." A dirty tunnel of smoke leaves her mouth and chugs upwards.

"And you definitely didn't notice this?"

"No." She flicks her cigarette, still glowing, into the garden. She sounds less certain now which is why she refuses to look at them.

David stands guard beside his wife. He's tall, taller than Mac, and I realise if they wanted to take Jonah, we'd have to fight them to get him back.

"So, what are you saying?" Mum asks.

"I'm saying, did you actually look at it properly before you accused my son of assaulting his baby?"

"Marian." Her husband touches her shoulder. She pulls away. Hugs Jonah tighter.

"No, David, I'm not having it. I'm not having her accuse Mac of something he hasn't done. He loves this baby. A damn sight more—"

"Marian!"

Cut short, she kisses Jonah on the forehead. On his Bindi mark. His strawberry naevus. "He's not in any pain," she says, more to herself than to anyone else in the room. "If you'd actually taken the time to look at him, you'd have realised that."

"I noticed it," I say, before I realise the words are waiting to be exposed.

"Okay, give him back." Mum glares at me and gestures to Marian to hand Jonah over. She rubs at the back of her head subconsciously, at where she landed on the coffee table, narrow grooves around her pinched mouth.

Marian stands her ground clutching Jonah to her chest. "Where's Mac now?" she asks.

"Don't know; don't care. I'll take the baby back now."

David steps forward. "Look, let's all just calm down. The

baby is our main concern right now. That's the reason you called us, isn't it?"

Mum doesn't look at him. "I'm not standing here being told I don't know my own baby. That mark wasn't there earlier, and now it is. If you're not going to help you might as well leave."

I don't know why she called them. I don't know why she called them and not Gran. Gran always remains calm in situations, like when her boyfriends' leave us, and Gran moves in with a small suitcase, and she cooks shepherd's pie and curry out of a jar and fills the newly sterilised fridge with food.

I can almost taste the silver daggers in the air, feel the breath struggling to feed her angry lungs, and then I realise why she called the skinny grandparents. This isn't about Jonah. She's barely glanced at him despite the fact her arms are reaching out to take him from Marian. This is about Mac, about getting back at him for whatever he's done to upset her. Maybe it's because, while she's been slipping in and out of our lives like a silent python sleeping, feeding, and hunting, he's created a position for himself, built a throne and placed a king-of-the-castle crown upon his own head. She wanted it, only now it's happened she doesn't like it.

"I'm not leaving until this is sorted," Marian says.

"Actually, you'll leave when I say you're leaving," Mum snaps back.

I want to shout at her, *You need to get Jonah back first*, because it's as if she's plunged into the sea at midnight wondering which way is up to the surface, kicking out at anything that gets in her way.

But David steps in, luckily. "Okay, this isn't achieving anything. If Marian says this is a strawberry naevus, I believe her, but for the avoidance of doubt, why don't we get an appointment booked in with the doctor or the health visitor, eh? What do you say, Lizzie?"

She rolls her eyes, says, "Fine," but makes no attempt to grab our baby back.

"Shall I call the doctor and you try to get hold of Mac?" David asks.

"No way I'm calling that bastard," she says, because she's used to having the last word.

29

It's eleven days before Mac returns.

His phone was switched off for the first few days, and when she tried calling Danielle there was no answer. This is what happens, I think, when you dig a hole and two people jump in together—whoever climbs out first has to decide whether to lend the other one a hand or leave them stranded and hope they don't make it, because if they do, they'll definitely grass you up on the other side. I don't tell her that, when he switched his phone back on, he was messaging me to check that Jonah was okay. I don't tell her because she doesn't ask.

He's different when he comes back. He has phone-secrets, quiet conversations on the balcony, tossing the occasional glance over his shoulder in case one of us has snuck up on him. In the evenings he's jumpy, twitchy, like his legs are suddenly too long for the sofa. With Jonah, nothing has changed, he's still as gentle and as caring as he was before, maybe more so, like potentially he stands to lose the one person who means the most to him in the world. I don't know what Marian and David said to him, but however they dressed it up, there's no mistaking the animosity between him and my mum.

Sucking up to him, she cooks his favourite meals, pours

a beer for him when he walks through the door after work, pretends she wants to go see the latest Marvel movie together. And he nods along, vacant-eyed, a Mac-hologram who exists for real somewhere else, somewhere we're not. At first, I think she must realise what she's done, how she's pushed too far this time. But with the return of Mac, comes the return of Danielle.

They buddy up in the kitchen with the secret burner phone, glug Coke from plastic tumblers, hold entire whisper-conversations, only surfacing when they remember some new gossip about someone they know. Gossip is for shouting out loud. Anyone can join in. Well, anyone but me because I've become the unpaid babysitter.

In the living room I'm stuck with *Go* bloody *Jetters,* and *PJ* bloody *Masks.* Franco brings me some green figure and says, "Gekko," like I'm supposed to know what he means. "Gekko." He puts it in my hand, his bottom lip rolled out. I throw it across the room. He fetches it back. "Gekko."

"I don't bloody want your Gekko," I say, and throw it again.

He fetches it like a puppy chasing a ball. I don't know if he thinks it's a game, but the third time he brings it back he stands in front of me, chubby belly sticking out, and holds onto the toy. I don't know why I think of it, but I imagine Jonah old enough to walk, trying to play with Danielle. I picture her ignoring him, tossing his toys away because she can't be bothered to play, and him crying silent lonely tears because he can't tell her what he wants. It seems like since Cee broke my heart, the cracks in what's left of it allow in all the hurt and pain and sadness I never saw before, each moment spooning away another little chunk of flesh.

I still have the pills in my room that came from Franco's

pocket. I can't believe Danielle left them laying around where he could find them. What if he'd swallowed one? What if . . . what if it had killed him? I'm going to show Mac when things settle down.

There's a green toy car on the floor. "Fetch your car," I say to Franco, gently this time. "We'll sit your Gekko in it."

I get dressed. I hear Mum on the phone to Gran slagging off Mac, how he's not interested in anyone but himself, how she doesn't trust his mate Slingo who Mac pops out to meet every evening, and how he doesn't seem to sit still for more than five minutes at a time.

Pot, kettle, and black spring to mind.

I can hear Gran's words without being able to hear her voice. "You've tried so hard with him, Lizzie," and, "He don't know which side his bread's buttered, that one," and, "He needs to stop and think about that baby."

"And he knows I'm so exhausted with the baby," she adds while she's on a roll.

I get the buggy ready and put Jonah in it, with a touchy-feely material book that Marian bought him when he was born. "I'm taking the baby out," I say.

"Where are you going?" she asks. "Hang on, Mum."

"Out."

"Pick me up a hair dye. Take a tenner out of my purse." She smiles at her telephone conversation like she's just stepped out of prison on a sunny day. "Summer's taking the baby out."

"Oh, she's a good girl," Gran will be saying.

With the buggy in front of me I don't have to watch where

I'm going. He sleeps as soon as we get outside and the air kisses his cheeks, wriggling until he gets comfortable and closing his eyes, drifting off in a blink of a moment. I can stare at him, pretend he's mine. Two girls in my year at school have already had babies. Tia will have another little girl by the end of the year. I miss Bliss with her cute little button nose and her blonde curls, but I wonder how long it'll be before she's parenting her own baby sister. I should've stayed in the woods with Cee when we had the chance. We could've been a hundred miles away by now, expert hunters and world class chefs of common plants and weeds, following the stars at night and sleeping, like animals, during the day. The world would've been ours. And no children.

But even as I imagine us with grubby faces, munching on a skewered squirrel with wild strawberries for pudding, I understand it's too late. I'm in too deep. I could no more abandon Jonah than I could've abandoned Cee. I blink back tears. There isn't a day goes by now when I don't cry. I'm like a sponge in a bucket perpetually filled with water.

At home, another note lies on the doormat. It gives me the evil eye as I wheel the buggy over it and into the living room, where I get Jonah out and set him down on the changing mat to have a kick about. In the kitchen Mum has left a note too:

Bitch-features has been kicking off again
Meeting Gran for a glass of wine.

I heat up a bottle of milk for Jonah. Change his bum. Shuffle my Spotify playlist. And still the white devil by the front door is grinning at me because it knows what I'm doing. I pick it up, smooth it out, and read it before I feed Jonah.

STAY AWAY. DON'T MAKE US KEEP YOU AWAY.

She must've said something to the Ovary. We've not had so many threats the past couple of weeks, since the big fight; I'd almost believed they'd gone away. Two days till the lantern ceremony. That's forty-eight hours plus a few as I guess they'll have a celebration first and set them off in the dark—they won't be as pretty in daylight. It makes me think of *Tangled*. Cee would love it, and I've been meaning to buy a lantern to take to the top of the hill by the woods, our favourite place; I know if I release it there, she'll be waiting.

STAY AWAY. DON'T MAKE US KEEP YOU AWAY.

Us? Who's helping the Ovary? Cee was close to her cousins but not close enough for them to be there for her when she was stuck with the kids. I try to hear the words spoken in the Ovary-drawl and it doesn't ring true in my head. Where are the swear words, the bitches, and bollocks, and bastards? Nah it's not right. And it's only now it dawns on me that the Ovary would've been banging on the door and causing the biggest scene ever, even if it meant the neighbours calling the police.

A puddle of sweat pools beneath Jonah's head where it rests on my arm. I don't know how long I sit on the sofa, Jonah asleep, the bottle teat wetting his bottom lip. I need to confront her, but that will only give her more ammunition against me, accusing her of bullying while she's still grieving. But if she is behind all this, Ritchie will know about it too.

The room at the top of our house is used for storage. There are black bags filled with unfashionable clothes and accessories, bits of toys, and jigsaw puzzles with missing pieces, Christmas decorations and three artificial trees, only one of which we use because the other two are tatty and the wrong shade of green. There's a hamster cage complete with sawdust and red plastic spinning wheel. The pink scooter Joe bought me, is propped up in one corner, its wonky wheel wedged between a dusty purple broken-zipped suitcase and a buckled box of Wii games. Occasionally the door is opened, and another bag of stuff tossed inside, but otherwise, we pretend the house ends at the living room ceiling.

A cabin bed built into the window wall is useful for climbing outside. That night, I ease myself backwards and up onto the dingy blue and white striped mattress and test the window lock. It opens easily. It's how Cee got out of the house the night I called her.

I'm dressed for the part anyways, head-to-toe in black. My roots are so grown out there's barely any blonde left, only my natural murky-water-brown, so I doubt anyone will spot me. It's a bright night. I think of all the nights me and Cee used to come out here with a bottle of gin and a packet of fags, and it feels like forever ago. My new forever consists of action movies and fourteen-hour sleeps; I can't even remember the last time I fake-tanned, and Jonah will eventually lose his baby-smell and turn into a little boy with scrappy knees and a devious grin, and no time for his big sister. And then I'll have no one.

Ritchie's always out. Most of the time he kipped on the sofa, Cee said, like he didn't need a full night's sleep in a bed with a mattress and pillows and a duvet, a few hours in a rabbit hole would keep him functioning. You could tell by the hollows beneath his eyes though, dug-out, and bruised. Vampire eyes. I'll wait all night if I must.

The grass is damp, so I sit cross-legged on the garden wall of the end house, camouflaged by the night, folding, and unfolding my legs. From here, I can view the streets lower down the hill, the road leading from the station, and the edge of the woods.

I don't have to wait long. It's the tip of his cigarette I spot first, glowing red for danger, a tiny spotlight bobbing along the ramp towards the walkway and home. His keys jingle as he drags them from the pocket of his leather jacket.

I jump down, landing in front of him.

"What the fuck!" He falters, head jerked back. "Summer?" He squints at me in the eerie light from the streetlamp. "You look different."

I'm not wearing makeup. Before, I wouldn't have been seen dead without makeup, the full works: foundation, concealer, contouring, mascara, brows, lipstick. Now it doesn't matter.

"Thanks," I say. I can tell by his face it wasn't a compliment, but I don't care. My nails are chipped, my back-tooth aches, and even though after my walk with Jonah, I napped for three hours, I could sleep till next month.

"Over here." He waves me into the shadows. I follow without question; I'm not scared of Ritchie. I smell cigarettes on his breath, the animal of his leather jacket, alcohol, garlic, and perfume. I try not to visualise him with one of his other girls. They're not here right now and anyways, he's probably already had another four or five girls I'm not aware of since I last saw him. Right now, he's here with me and that's what matters.

He doesn't build up to what he has to say, just dives right in. "Look, Summer, you can't come. You know that, right?"

His words are a knife-tip, teasing the arteries of my heart, screwing them like noodles around a chopstick ready to drag out and toss away; but I park the pain for now. I want to hear the truth.

"I know."

He holds my arms, stares intently at me and I realise the slant of his eyes is the same as Cee's, the curve of his top lip is hers too. I can't differentiate between them, between the love I feel, felt, for them both. They're the same person to me. They always were. The realisation that she lives on in her big brother is so overwhelming I can't breathe, my chest aching with the effort of pumping blood to my agitated brain.

30

"You know?" He drops my arms, puts his keys away, and taps another cigarette into the palm of his hand, lighting it with a match. For a moment the flame highlights his cheekbones with golden fire, and I remember how it felt to kiss him while lightning inflamed the sky, and rain drenched our clothes. He blows smoke over his shoulder and away from me. "So why do you keep telling everyone you'll be there?"

"Have I said I'll be there?"

He blinks, glances away, shifts his weight from one foot to the other. "Well, yeah, your mum said . . ."

"I don't care what my mum said."

He sucks on the end of his cigarette. I wish he would smile. Their smiles, so guarded, so rationed to special occasions, are one and the same; if Ritchie would only smile, I could see her again, I know I could.

He flicks the cigarette onto the pavement at his feet where it glows briefly, a tiny dying fire. I shiver. It isn't cold but his silence is so final, I feel him slipping him away from me, fading in front of my eyes, being sucked into the universe with his sister, extinct together. It feels like goodbye.

But then he grabs my hand and I'm jolted back to now. "Come with me," he says in a low voice.

My heart is thumping, and I've gone from shivering to being overheated, like I've suddenly stepped off a plane in a hot faraway land. His hand trembles. He's cold or nervous maybe. Ritchie isn't the kind of person you expect to be nervous; he's the kind of person who takes control, who the other lads look up to, the one who protects, and guides, and praises, even when his own life doesn't quite cut it. And because of this quiet confidence, everyone follows. I follow him now.

He doesn't look at me. Head down, a few steps, and we're at their front door. He lets us in. I've never been inside their house before. I hold my breath. I'm half-expecting Cee to jump out and say, "Close your eyes, the place is a mess."

It's dark in their hallway, the same as ours but different because our light is always on, and this is a night-version, with strange lumpy shadows. Still holding my hand, Ritchie bypasses the kitchen and heads upstairs.

Their top room is empty besides a bed built below the wide window shelf the same as ours. He doesn't switch the light on. Inside, he turns, cups my face with both hands and kisses me, nudging the door closed behind my back. I can taste cigarettes and beer, and rain from a summer storm, when two people kissed on the grass and he made me feel like I was something special.

"A summer storm for my Summer," he'd said.

"I love you," I'd said with the innocent trust of first love. In all good romcoms, a declaration of love is reciprocated, with tender kisses and bear-hugs, and I'd expected at least one of these from Ritchie. But all he'd done was roll over, pull me close and kiss my forehead, and tell me I was his Summer. That must have meant something surely. If it meant nothing, then why are we here now, in his house, his lips on mine?

My chest is ready to explode. All my senses confused by the sensation of his lips on mine, so when he lifts my jumper over my head, I don't even make it easy for him, but wait for my head to reappear, puppet-like and crazy-haired. The buttons of my jeans pop open easily. He kneels on the carpet at my feet and slides them down over my hips. Grabbing my buttocks with both hands he pulls me close and kisses me through my pants.

I can't open my eyes. I don't want to see what he's doing, I don't want to see the top of his head, my shaking knees, the alien bed under the window. But most of all I don't want to spoil the moment. I don't know how we end up on the floor but for a while, the lantern ceremony, the wedding, the car crash, all vanish, and I finally understand my love for Ritchie and Cee. They both get me. Without them in my life, and with my spine bared to the world for anyone to stab, I can't view what's ahead of me. I can't take a step forward. I can't even breathe right.

This is love. If this were a movie moment, we'd be in the back of a vintage car in the belly of the Titanic, windows steamed from our body heat and beneath us, an old blanket that might have been made from magical golden feathers. I keep my eyes closed and pretend I'm someone else, somewhere else, and this is the first night of the rest of our lives.

Ritchie doesn't use protection. He doesn't mention it and I don't care; all I care about is his weight on top of me, the smell of him, the way it feels to be filled to the brim with him. If the Ovary stomped up the stairs and barged in on us, I'd no more notice her than the carpet burns on my back, or the spindly-legged spiders guarding the corners of the window frame. I hold on to him and wait for the storm.

After, on the roof, with the stars twinkling and happy above our heads, he holds me close, my face buried in his neck. This is, I think, how I want to spend the rest of my life. When we're together no one else can touch me. I start to weave a life for us, in a little flat at the edge of the woods, Ritchie returning home from work in his leather jacket, me stirring a homemade Bolognese sauce on the hob while Jonah stacks plastic cups on the floor in the living room. We'd have photographs of Cee in silver frames on the wall, and in the evenings, we'd laugh about the chaos and the drama we caused as teenagers.

Anyways I have it all planned. I can smell his shampoo, and our dinner, and baby powder, I can even hear *Gavin and Stacey* on the telly, a train jolting the window frames as it passes on its approach to the station, kids kicking a ball against a metal garage door.

STAY AWAY. DON'T MAKE US KEEP YOU AWAY.

The words jump in front of my eyes, unexpected, and my breathing becomes light and rapid. Of course, the Ovary wasn't writing the notes—she didn't need to because she had Ritchie to write them for her.

"I know you wrote the notes," I say, my voice catching in my throat.

I don't move. Our entire happy-ever-after depends on me protecting this moment, and accepting Ritchie's apology, which is sure to follow because this is our cinema moment, and nothing can spoil it. Any moment now.

I know he heard me because his shoulders have tensed rigid and he pulls me even closer into his side, both arms circling my bare shoulders, my lips and nose pressed so hard against his skin I can't breathe. I try to regulate my breathing, stay completely still.

"I'm sorry, Summer," he says finally.

Right words, right order. But, the delay, the slow release of breath at the end of the sentence, and I know there's a 'but' coming.

"I didn't know what else to do."

How about not write them in the first place? Or speak to me about it instead of running away whenever he saw me coming? One warning could be forgotten, heat of the moment, overwhelmed by the realisation his sister is never coming back, fury fuelled by grief. But more than one? Two. Five. Ten. Multiple threats are premeditated—that is what they call it. They're planned, deliberate, thought through with the specific end-result in mind.

"I was looking for someone else to blame," he continues. "It was bad enough she was gone. But the way she went. The heart problem." His chest is so still I slip my hand, like a caterpillar, across his ribs to check he's still breathing. His lungs are filling with starry air, barely. "As a baby, you know, I knew she was ill because of the times we had to visit her in hospital. She'd be all wrapped up in tubes and the kids in the other beds all looked worse and scared me because they had limbs missing, and no hair, and Jesus it was so hard, but I was only like three years old. And then she got better, and she was just another kid going to school and wanting to be a pop star. And most of the time she was fucking annoying. But I loved her. I did." With the last words he squeezes my back like he's trying to convince me, like I need to believe him.

"I know," is all I can manage right now, and my voice is croaky with tears.

"I'd never have done anything to hurt her. Fuck knows she only wanted someone to look after her."

This, I think, isn't entirely true. She didn't want to be looked after, because she believed she was strong enough to look after herself. What she wanted was a break, a future, magical adventures and music and laughter, and she believed that Ritchie would be the one to whisk her away and give her everything she dreamed of.

"The pills were only meant to give her a buzz."

I hold my breath, my stomach turning to sludge.

"I'd shared them with her before. She said it was better than booze, made her happier. And nothing bad happened before so why would it be different this time?" His body is shaking, and I force my eyes open, raise my head from his shoulder to check I'm hearing what I think I'm hearing. He's crying. Tears streak his cheeks, crawling down the side of his face and into his ears, the curve of his neck, my chest where it's pressed against him all sweaty and hot.

"Ritchie," I whisper. I need to hear him say it, but at the same time, I wish I'd never come here. "Which pills are you talking about?"

"That night," he says. "I gave her the pills that killed her. It was me, Summer. I killed my baby sister."

The sobs that shudder through him are noisy, heart-breaking;

I wait, breathless, for the sound of cracking ribs and splintering spine. I should hold him, but I feel fragile, like a sparrow beside this mountain of grief. I'm still trying to understand what he's telling me and until I do, I'm not entirely sure I want to hold him.

So, I wait. I wait for him to dissolve, and dry out, and mend the broken pieces of his heart, while I think about what he's told me. He gave Cee the pills that night. He gave them to her, knowing she had a heart problem, and then when she died, and the Ovary decided to blame me, he went along with it.

I jerk upright and scrabble on the tiles beneath me for my jumper. I can't look at his naked body, his hairy legs, and his stubby feet, the soles so pale in the moonlight. What was tonight all about? Did he think it would make me feel better? A consolation prize? *Yeah, sorry about the crap through the letterbox, I love ya really*. He was supposed to look out for us. He was supposed to be different. He was strong, confident, a bad boy with a heart; it's why he found it so easy to get all the girls. But all this time he'd been letting me take the blame for his guilt.

"Why haven't you told anyone?" I say, and my voice is blunt. "Why didn't you tell the police?"

He sighs, and in that moment, I hate him. "What good would it have done? It wouldn't have brought her back." He sits up, finds his cigarettes in his jacket pocket, and lights up. "I wish I could take it back, Summer. I wish I could change it. I wish I'd never bought them." He offers me a drag and I shake my head.

"If you tell the police, they can arrest the dealer," I say. It's not much but it's better than doing nothing. Tom will still face charges of reckless driving, but he won't be able to accuse me of supplying Cee with the pills that killed her, because the police will have the proof. I think this through, emotionless, empty, like I'm doing some problem solving in math class. Nothing will bring her back, but if we're to ever breathe normally again, all the frayed ends need to be knotted and secure in the knowledge that we did what we could.

"It's complicated," he says, head hanging low, eyes focused on his shadow-feet.

"You're protecting someone."

"Leave it, Summer." He's gathering clothes. He hands me my jeans and suddenly the suspicion that Cee might be watching, judging me, is overwhelming and I need to get away from here.

"Who was it?" I ask, shimmying my pants back up. Their wetness feels odd between my legs.

He shakes his head, makes no effort to dress.

"It's the least you can do," I say. "I can go to the police with the threats, tell them it was you. There'll be fingerprints on the notes." A far worse idea enters my head, one I'd never considered until Mac put it out there, but I blurt it out now without a thought for the consequences. "And I'm still only fifteen you know."

He doesn't look at me. I realise if he ever had any feelings for me, I've dragged them out, kicked them to death, and buried them beneath the tallest tower in the farthest corner of the planet, but I can't think about that until I'm back home. Right now, I need an answer for Cee's sake.

He swallows, drags his T-shirt over his head. "It was Mac."

31

I show Mac the notes. I spread them out across the table like when Gran is playing Patience with a deck of cards. Mum has gone shopping; at least, that's what she told us. I watch Mac's eyes flickering across them, soaking up the words.

"You kept them?" he says.

"Cee's brother was sending them."

"Ritchie?"

I swallow. All this time I believed Mac only knew Ritchie and the Ovary to nod to in passing, and now he mentions his name, like I was the one who was blind, not him. I want to blurt it out in a hurry, get it over and done with, let Mac know that I know, but part of me doesn't want to be guilty of ruining what we have. For Jonah's sake.

So, I lie. "He thought I gave Cee the pills. Everyone thinks I'm guilty of giving her the pills that killed her."

I hold my breath, chew my bottom lip, tears stinging behind my eyes while I wait for him to accept responsibility. If he owns up now, I can forgive him, I think. We can start afresh, the four of us. I'll never stop loving Cee, but I know I have to live my life, with or without her.

"Summer, no one thinks you gave her the pills."

My stomach twists and I feel sick. He's going to deny it all the way. "Tom, the guy who was driving the car, he thinks I did. He messaged me to say I'd better confess because he's not going down for it."

"He can't prove it." Mac's eyes are still on the notes. "It'll be his word against yours."

"And I took them too," I say. I wait for him to speak, but his eyelids flicker back and forth across the capital letters on the scraps of paper in front of us, and it dawns on me that he could have stopped all this because he knew all along that I wasn't guilty. "I want to go to the lantern ceremony."

"Summer . . ." He looks at me now. "Let it go. You don't need to send a lantern into the sky to remember your friend. You said so yourself. You're vulnerable right now. Don't put yourself into a situation which will make you feel even worse than you already do."

He gathers the notes into a pile, hands them to me, his fingers lingering on mine. For a while we are both silent and then his phone pings, and he reads a message.

"I just need to make a call." He goes out the front door, his phone already pressed to his ear, and it's a few seconds before I wonder why he didn't want to make this call on the veranda.

I stare at the ceiling, at a cobweb floating like a jellyfish between the lampshade and the curtain pole. My brain feels anaesthetised, straitjacketed, so individual cells can be picked out and stamped on, the thoughts I really should be organising in my head, smashed into tiny, confused pieces.

Ritchie was sending the notes to save his own skin. Honestly that's the least of my problems now; I can't even deal with thinking about them. I'll go to the police if I must, although it's unlikely we'll be receiving more.

Ritchie supplied Cee with pills. She never said that's where she got them although I probably never asked. Ritchie was a god to Cee; she trusted him, she worshipped him, she adored him. If he'd told her to blow up the school because the headmaster was a wrong'un who touched up little boys, she'd have done it. No questions asked. So, if he said he had pills that'd give her a buzz, a buzz is what she'd have expected to get.

Ritchie got the pills from Mac. I never saw this one coming. But now the fact is out there, I can't un-see it, and the more I think about it, the more I can see Mac shoving a hand in his pocket and producing a tiny packet of pills for a tenner or whatever. He's hardwired. A back-tooth-crunching toffee. Apart from when he's with Jonah, but now he's back, even that gooey centre has changed. It's solidified into a kind of resolution, a kind of 'this is my son, he has Down's syndrome and I'll do everything I can to help him, but I'm still Mac the hard man.'

When I think about that night, I remember coming home from the park without Cee, Mac standing in the kitchen in his Tommy Hilfiger T-shirt, the front door closing behind him as I went downstairs to my room. Is that when he met Ritchie? Another thought judders through me making me blink. The packet of pills in Franco's pocket that I assumed had been Danielle's––did Franco find them here? What if that had been Jonah? I don't know what to do.

Ritchie wanted everyone to believe it was my fault because he knew if he snitched on Mac, he'd be dragged down with him. He wanted *me* to believe it was my fault. And I did. I accepted the blame with veins sliced open, with grown-out roots and chipped nails and then . . . tears well in my eyes at the vision . . . we had sex in the room at the top of their house. He knew how much I liked him, and it was probably his way of thanking me for carrying the blame. My heart is tapping in my chest and my throat is sore with all the stored-up tears. He doesn't even like me. I'm just a kid who used to hang out with his little sister.

I still blame myself. If I hadn't begged Cee to come out with us, she wouldn't have jumped off the roof, or accepted pills from Ritchie, or filled a water bottle with gin. She wouldn't have swallowed the pills that killed her. She was asleep. I woke her up, whined and pleaded and made her feel bad because I'd realised too late, I didn't want to be alone in a car with two guys I barely knew, and she came because she had my back. If I'd not called her, she'd have woken up the next morning another day older. If I'd called her and not kicked off like a selfish little twat, she'd have woken up the next morning another day older. But Ritchie gave her the pills. And Mac sold Ritchie the pills.

If I tell the police, there's a possibility he'll go to jail. Mum will hate me. An image of a feather boa wrapped around her neck springs to mind. She'll hate me for being a snitch, but far worse than snitch-status, is the very real possibility that Jonah will hate me for losing his dad.

Jonah. He deserves better.

I can hear the exercise bike humming through the ceiling. Mac in the kitchen cooking breakfast, the smell of bacon making me feel queasy. Music on the telly: Ed Sheeran. When I hear Mac yell from the front door, "I'm popping out," I jump out of bed, yank on my jeans and a vest, and fly up the stairs, grabbing Mum's flip-flops from the porch as I follow him. He's already crossing the road towards the railway station, face turned towards the sky like he's owning the day, and any doubts I had fly away.

"Mac!" I yell.

He turns to face me, eyes narrowed, but he waits for me to catch him up.

When I'm standing in front of him, my breathing shallow, one flip-flop half hanging off my foot, I say, "I know you gave Ritchie the pills."

He looks at me and his expression doesn't change. I don't know what I expected, full-on tears like Ritchie or what, but it wasn't this. "What do you want me to say, Summer?" He shrugs.

I blink back hot stinging tears and swallow. "The pills killed Cee."

He glances around and then grabs my arm, his fingers digging into my flesh, and drags me into the nearest alleyway where he lets me go but keeps me in his sight like I might run for it.

I rub my arm and wait for him to speak.

When he speaks his voice is low so that it doesn't travel. "She knew the risks, Summer. You both did. You want to play grown-up games; you accept the consequences."

I can't believe it. I look into his eyes and they're empty, hard, cruel; this isn't the same man I believed would stick around forever, would look out for me, promise me everything would be alright. It can't be.

"That's it?" I shake my head. "That's all you have to say?"

"What else is there?" He takes a packet of cigarettes from

his pocket and lights one, cupping his hands around it gently. He inhales and blows a trail of smoke above our heads. His voice softens, "Look, Summer, I get it. You're angry, you're grieving, you're hurt, but nothing is going to bring her back. All you can do is hold on to your memories, remember the fun you had, and learn from it."

He straightens and I hadn't even realised that his face was close to mine, but the distance between us jolts me back to reality.

"I could tell the police," I blurt out.

He stares at me then as if he doesn't recognise me. "And then what? What about Jonah? You want him to suffer too?"

He's playing the guilt-card because he knows I love my baby brother, but this isn't fair. None of this is fair.

"Everyone was blaming me, and you didn't say anything. You–"

"I was trying to protect you!" He's almost yelling now. "I told you to stay away from them. I told your mum to let it go, but she wouldn't listen either."

"No, Mac." I can see it now. All the times he told me and Mum to stay away from the funeral, the lantern ceremony, the wedding reception, he wasn't thinking about me, he was thinking about himself. I wonder if he has threatened to take Ritchie down with him if it gets out. Probably. "You were protecting yourself."

He flicks ash from the cigarette, inhales again, and watches me coolly. "You think your mum will be happy without me? Go and tell her then, but I won't walk away from my son without a fight."

Mac doesn't glance behind him as he walks away, of course

he doesn't, his strides are confident, strong. It only takes a moment for me to decide to follow him. I keep a distance between us all the same, dropping to my knees behind a car when he crosses the road, and speeding up when he turns the corner at the bottom of the road. At the station, he waits in the car park, lights up another cigarette, makes a call. I can't get close enough to listen although I can hear the low murmur of his voice, but when he squashes the butt beneath his trainer, and slips through the side entrance onto the platform, I dart through the stationhouse garden, leaping over the flowerbeds that say DO NOT TOUCH, and crouch behind a bin that reeks of dog shit.

Mac hangs back. Aside from the fact I didn't see him buy a ticket, it's obvious he isn't waiting to get on the train: he doesn't glance along the track or check his watch or the board every two minutes. He's chilling and killing, knee bent, one foot propping up the wall.

I can guess who he's waiting for as soon as she steps off the train. She has dark hair in waves almost down to her waist, a tan, maybe mixed race, huge dark eyes, and a Radley bag slung over her shoulder. Her smile is all for Mac. She closes her eyes when he kisses her.

I swallow. I feel the betrayal like a punch in the stomach. Not my betrayal, not Mum's, but Jonah's. His son. How could he do this to his beautiful baby?

His arm slips around her waist as they walk away, and I watch through hot frustrated tears.

32

We're pissed before the dresses arrive for our final fitting. Tia's mum brought bottles of Prosecco and Chambord because her granddaughters, Tia's nieces, are stroppy little fuckers, and we'd all need a drink to keep calm.

They're noisy. But they're not as noisy as us. Tia's laugh can probably be heard the other side of town, and Frankie brought all kinds of Ann Summers' freebies—her auntie is a party organiser—so they've been on their knees, blindfolded and hands secured behind their back with pink fluffy handcuffs, attempting to pass a black dildo to each other using only their mouths. I laugh with the rest of them while I picture Mac and his bitch doing the same thing.

I'm grateful for the noise. I laugh because they expect me to. I knock back the Prosecco and hold my glass out for a refill, hoping they don't notice my nails; the last set of acrylics I gnawed away at until they fell off and my nails are crap now, bitty and rough. First thing they said when I walked in was, I look tired and what had I been up to? I hinted at seeing some new geezer. It's what they expected.

The giggles, and the music, and the conversation, swirl around me and I think I might suffocate if I don't get out of here soon. The nieces, Aston and Molly, sit on the sofa with their phones, rolling their eyes at us and whispering behind their hands like we won't guess they're gossiping about us. They remind me of the popular girls in school; they used to hang around the art room with Mr Whittaker at lunchtimes because they knew he wouldn't send them outside, and they'd message each other across the table about all the girls they didn't like.

When the woman finally brings the dresses zipped up in white covers, we all pile into Tia's bedroom to change. They're baby pink, strapless, down to the floor. My bodice feels loose like my nips will pop out if I breathe.

"You need some tit-tape, babe," Tia says.

"She needs a meat pie," her mum says.

I laugh. Shrug. Keep my arms by my side while the woman sticks pins in me. They don't know my head is spinning around the moon. The Prosecco has affected me more than it ever has before but I've not eaten today, and I can't remember what I ate yesterday.

"You need to look after yourself, sweetheart," Tia's mum says. "I know it's been tough, but you need to think about yourself now. After the lantern ceremony tonight, you can look forward to the wedding without all that hanging over you." She waves a hand in front of her face to indicate the 'all that' as something to be swatted away like a fly, or an unwanted leaflet.

Frankie widens her eyes at Tia.

"You're gabbing, Mum," Tia says.

"Oh, it's the Prosecco. I'm sure it'll be a lovely turnout tonight though, eh?"

"She can't keep her trap shut." Tia zips the back of Frankie's dress. "Summer isn't going," she says over the other girl's shoulder.

"Oh, why not? It's a lovely way to say goodbye to your friend."

I wish they would all shut up. They speak about Cee like she's got the train to London and will be back when her purse is empty. Their lives haven't changed. They don't have a Cee-shaped hole through which they bleed at night, only to wake up a bite size smaller each morning. They have someone to chat to in bed. They're not scared to set off a Chinese bloody lantern in case someone kicks off at them. Maybe I should go. Let them all kick off and I'll set the record straight.

"And it's for a good cause," she's still speaking. "My brother Jimmy had a heart attack, he did, only forty-two he was. Amazing what they can do nowadays though. Surgeons fixing heart problems like they're wiring a plug."

"Mum, leave it," Tia snaps.

"What? She can come with us. You come with us, sweetheart. Our Don's going to get a curry on the way home, make a night of it."

"Are you done?" I ask the woman who still has pins in her mouth. I'm tugging the dress down over my hips anyway.

Aston and Molly snigger, heads together, like they've never seen a pair of tits before.

"Summer, you don't have to go," Tia says.

"I know."

"I'm just about there," says the woman on the floor.

I drag my clothes on ignoring the hair smothering my face. There's no noise now, like they want my disappearance to be loud and messy so they can chew it up and spit it out over the next few bottles, and behind my back, without feeling guilty. Quiet is bad.

"What did I say?" her mum asks as I snatch my bag from the kitchen counter and leave.

The house is quiet save for the hum of the fridge, although I can't tell if the sound is inside my head, a product of the several glasses of pink frothy bubbles I knocked back, or if it's buzzing through the machine.

My head spins a little as I peep into the kitchen. No one's there.

"Mum?" I yell.

I wonder if they've taken Jonah out for a walk, or to Gran's, or the park or something. But I don't know if Mac came back, or if he's still shacked up somewhere with train-tramp. My stomach rumbles like it knows telepathically I'm standing in the room with the food.

There's not much in the fridge, butter, cheese slices, a scrape of jam in the bottom of a sticky jar and half a carton of milk. Cereal it is then. I reach for the cornflakes and tip the box over with my clumsy fingers taking the Weetabix with it. I wait for the thud of the secret phone. But it's gone. Good! Maybe she's ended it with whoever she's been cracking on with. I should've told Mac when I had the chance, but I still believed Mac was the best thing that had ever happened to her. To us. To Jonah. Now, I can't even remember who that girl was.

Milk dribbles down my chin as I miss my mouth with the spoon; I can't even eat properly today. I'm pissed that everyone is going tonight but me. I'm pissed at Mac for cheating on us because that's what we are, an us—if he cheats on my mum, he cheats on me and Jonah too. I'm pissed at Ritchie for being a coward when I'd always believed he had wings, someone destined for great things like Cee. I miss her so much my chest aches. I crunch cornflakes between my teeth, and I can't swallow; I cry tears that mingle with milk and saturate my chin, my neck, my chest; I gulp air and it battles its way straight back out of my lungs because it knows there's no reason for it to stay.

Four people in this house and there's not one of them I can reach out and touch with my fingertips. Not one of them I can talk to. This, I think, is what I miss most about Cee, the nights we'd stay awake chatting shit and still have stuff to say when morning came. I don't even know what we talked about, or how we didn't get sick of the sounds of our own voices, but we didn't; we'd have carried on chatting shit all through the day too if she didn't have babies to look after.

Maybe I should go tonight. It's a futile idea. I can picture it now, a hill full of people staring at the pretty lanterns in the sky, with me at the bottom, staring at the backs of peoples' heads, forgotten, like the last girl to be chosen for the netball team because everyone knows she can't score.

I wonder where the phone has gone. I wonder who Staffie is; I bet it's someone I know, or someone I'd recognise from the pub, or the leisure park. Most likely a bouncer, or pikey. Someone with attitude. And a dog. That makes me giggle. Why would you call yourself Staffie? He must be bald with muscles too big for his arms.

I guzzle a can of Diet Coke. The bubbles in my head subside a little leaving behind the promise of a grey evening in front of the telly with Jonah, sound turned up to smother my thoughts. I could message Kofi, see if he wants to come round with some cider and watch *Dirty Dancing*, but I'd probably end up telling him about Mac supplying the pills, and he'll get all deep on me, and talk about setting records straight, and karma, and doing it for Cee.

But what about Jonah? What about doing it for him too?

He has a right to love his dad without it being poisoned by my selfish need to vindicate myself. He has a right to a half-decent father, one who's happy to be hands-on, play mum *and* dad, get stuck in and learn sign language, and research ways to get the best help for his child. But what he doesn't need is a dad who's a drug dealer. There's only one way that's going to go and it isn't up. Surely a drug-dealer dad isn't better than no dad. My head is spinning.

I shower, wrap up in my princess dressing gown, and sprawl on the sofa with the remote. I've seen all the new movies on Netflix, and I'm done with bloody Marvel. I choose *Mamma Mia 2*, easy-watching and young Bill is peng, and nip back to the kitchen for another Diet Coke. It's only when I'm walking back into the living room that I spot a movement in the Moses basket. My heart thumps and my ears feel like they're going to burst. All I can think is, an animal, a cat or hedgehog or pigeon, has somehow got into the house and made itself at home in Jonah's crib.

Holding my breath, and my stomach, and the flaps of my dressing gown around me, I tiptoe a few steps across the room. A pink chubby hand appears above the side of the bed.

Jonah.

33

I reach the Moses basket in a millionth of a second and lift him out, still not quite believing it's really him.

"Hello, baby?" I say, as I nuzzle his neck. He smells of pee. His sleepsuit is damp on my hand. His head nestles against me, and he sucks on my collarbone with his wet gummy mouth.

I carry him to the top of the stairs. "Mum?" I yell. "MUM?"

There's no answer. From the fridge, I take the last bottle of milk, still holding Jonah, and set it in the bottle warmer. I take him downstairs, check her room, my room, the yard through the patio doors. Back to the kitchen and I wonder if she's upstairs with Mac, talking, or not talking, although I'd be able to hear them if there was anything else going on. I wander upstairs anyway. The top room is empty, and the house wears its loneliness like a weighted cloak dragged through the muddy puddles of a winter day.

My hand is cold and soggy, so I put Jonah on the changing mat and sort his wet nappy first before dressing him in a clean baby-grow. They say babies cry all the time but not our baby, I think.

"He's a happy little soul," Gran says.

I wonder how some souls are born happy, and some are too

busy complaining to even realise they're not happy, and others are born with misery at their core, even if they're bottle-fed on liquid gold and a ton of sparkling talent. Whatever Jonah's soul is made up of, it's pink, and pure, and honest, and he follows me with his eyes wide open and trusting.

Holding the end of the warmed bottle with my right hand, I find Mum's number on my phone with my left and hit the green button. The call goes through to voicemail and I leave a message: "Where are you?"

Every two minutes I call, and every two minutes she doesn't pick up. I message her on Facebook. *Where are u?* And on WhatsApp.

Nothing.

"It's okay," I say to Jonah, as if he can tell that it definitely isn't okay. But the more calls that go unanswered, the less certain I am about what's going on. The bubbly has evaporated from my brain with the cold realisation I'm in control of my baby brother, so that's one good thing, and I try to work out where she might be, and what might've tempted her to leave Jonah home alone. I know she's selfish but even so, he's a baby. Last thing she should want right now is police involvement in her life. My life. Mac's life.

She must be with Mac—he means the most to her. Maybe someone saw him with train-tramp and called her. Maybe Danielle heard the gossip, there's bound to be gossip, no one round here can survive without it, and they love nothing better than a nice deep cut, and a quick twist of a knife in the gut. If someone has seen them, bet your life, twenty-four hours and the whole estate will be chewing on it for breakfast.

I consider calling Mac, but the thought flits through my

brain and vanishes as quickly as it appeared. He didn't consider Jonah when he was at the train station so I'm not giving him the opportunity now. Gran's too far away. And Marian and David are too pushy. They'll take him away from me before I can blink.

I encourage Jonah to drink as much of his bottle as I can, slowly, because of his reflux issues, and sit him upright on my lap to wind him. Ten minutes, I think, and if I've not heard from her, I'll call Mac. Or I could just wait for them to come home, pretend Jonah wasn't left on his own. If I speak to Mac, explain why I'm worried, there'll be a huge row, a fuck-off spilling-blood fight, and I can't face it, not tonight. It's Cee's night. Even if I'm not invited. Maybe I could blackmail Mac over the pills. You don't mention her leaving Jonah alone, and I'll stay quiet about the pills.

Jonah burps loudly. "Good boy," I say, rubbing his back. His tongue rolls out and I smile at him, at his little Buddha belly, although I know he doesn't understand what a smile is.

I check my phone. Fifteen minutes have passed and no messages. I'll give her another five. Five minutes to check up on her baby, and then I'm calling Mac. Why should I protect her? She decided to have a baby; she must've known what was involved. She already had me.

I wish Cee was here because she'd know what to do. I stare at the patio doors, at the corner of the sofa, at the spot in front of the telly where she used to sit cross-legged with a magazine, and I can't see her. Jonah blinks heavily and closes his eyes. He's asleep within seconds.

I don't know what to do. Why hasn't one of them called me? I'm getting edgy, my brain cells jumpy, and tears lurking in my forehead waiting to spill. My head aches, probably from the booze. A message beeps on my phone. I pick it up with shaky fingers and open it. It's Kofi.

Sorry been quiet, lots going on. You ok? I worry about you Summer. Xx

I type a message and erase it, type again.

Lots going on here too. Came home and found Jonah on his own. Xx

Wtf?! I'm on my way. Xxx

No don't it's fine. We're all good. Xxx

I hit redial one last time. Still no answer. Kofi doesn't reply, and I picture him hunting under his bed for a pair of socks and trainers, pulling on sweatpants, picking up his cap on the way out. There's no time to think. She'll go ballistic if she finds out I've told Kofi, so I need to act quick. Scrolling through my contacts, I find Mac's number and hit the green button.

My heart is about to burst; my head is thumping. Three rings, and he picks up. Only, before he speaks, I hear a woman's voice in the background, giggling and easy, like she's on a picnic with a glass of M&S wine and some pre-washed strawberries.

"Hello?" Mac says. "Summer?"

I hang up.

The voice didn't belong to my mum.

This is shit. My tears drip onto Jonah's head, and I rub them away with the corner of his muslin. They don't care about us.

They're too busy fighting their own battles to help us triumph in ours. I don't deserve the Pandora necklace, or the 'baby girls' or the holographic acrylics, I realise that now. Everything the Ovary said about me was true. We shouldn't have been driving around in some guy's car in the middle of the night, popping pills and swigging gin; we should've been tucked up in bed, completed homework in our school bags, and uniform on the back of a chair, waiting to be worn the following morning. I should've left Cee in bed. If I wasn't so needy and desperate, I'd not have even called Cee. I'd have said no to the car-ride, and come home on my own, sober, kissed Jonah goodnight before I went to sleep, dreamed of beach holidays, and pretty neon-green bikinis looking hot against a suntan.

Growing up is crap. It's like having your eyes bleached squeaky clean, and finally noticing that the adults you loved and trusted, are not the people you thought they were. Jonah has all this to learn. I wish I could keep him in his perfect bubble, keep him like Peter Pan and the Lost Boys, in a world where shadows can be unstitched, and mermaids do exist.

I can't let this happen to him. They don't deserve a second chance with my baby brother, a second chance they'll screw up. They need to be taught a lesson. I let this new reasoning settle for a moment. I know I'm not perfect. I know I'm selfish, and difficult, and needy, but I also know that I would not have left Jonah on his own, not now, not after Cee.

If Kofi is on his way, I probably have about half an hour, twenty minutes if he catches the bus. He'll stop me. He'll be all practical and talk about food and money and heating and tell me to forget about what they've done. I don't hesitate. I place Jonah back in the Moses basket. Downstairs in my room, I throw on the clothes I wore to Tia's. In the bottom of the wardrobe, I find the leather tasselled rucksack Gran got me one birthday. In it, I shove a hoodie, a pair of jeans, some pants, and my toothbrush. From their room, I cram in as many nappies as I can, a tube of Bepanthen, and some baby wipes. Fuck! Jonah needs milk.

Running now, I fly into the kitchen, panting, take the bottles out of the steriliser, and use what's left in the kettle to measure out three bottles with four ounces equally. Four scoops of milk in each one. Thickener. Quick shake, Milk spills over my hands and the counter but I don't have time to wipe it.

The bag is so full it won't close, but I stow it under the buggy, fasten Jonah, tucking a fluffy blanket around him, and we're out the door.

It isn't until we reach the end of the road, I realise I don't have my keys, but it doesn't matter. We won't be needing them.

34

A short distance into the woods, I dump the buggy. It's not built for this. I sling the bag over my shoulder and carry Jonah. I know where I'm going. At least that's what I think when I start picking my way off the almost-path, and over crawling tree-roots and spiteful bushes. It's difficult when you're carrying a baby. God knows how they managed in caveman times, or did they strap the child to the back of an animal, and pray it was still alive when they reached their destination?

It's darker than I expected. As we left the house, fat, bruising, grey clouds started burying the sun and making way for the breeze, and already my fingers are starting to feel numb with cold. I've never felt it to this extent before, but today, because I'm holding Jonah, it almost feels like something out of a horror movie, you know, one of those where you blink and your mate disappears, only to turn up thirty minutes later, stripped naked and minus a head.

Don't think about it. Don't.

I'm heading the right way, I think, the river to my left, only when I arrive at what should be the giant oak with the twisted trunk and grassy roots, I discover I'm wrong, and the hollow behind the tree is nothing but a tangle of thorny bushes strangled by miles and miles of sticky weed. Three times I retrace my steps, almost back to where the buggy waits like an alien creature for the return of its mothership, my arms screaming with the weight of the baby, the bag jumping off my back with every footstep. It must be here. She wouldn't have gone and left me.

I stumble over a rock, or an animal, something I miss because I'm holding Jonah, and land awkwardly on my right hip and elbow, which I've stuck out at right angles to protect the baby. Jonah's head touches the ground with a gentle thud, and I'm immediately on my knees, cradling him close to me, kissing his forehead, and his face, and murmuring, "Okay, baby. It's okay, baby, I've got you."

He cries, a strange sound like a duckling quacking for its mother, or for food, and I rock him back and forth, bumping him up and down, the way Cee used to do with Demi when she fell over and cut her knee, and cried real painful tears. When he stops crying, I hold him away from me, ignoring the throbbing pain in my elbow, and study his face and head with my eyes and fingertips, searching for blood or a swelling lump. I find nothing.

We keep moving. I'm crying when we return to the oak, scared we'll be stumbling through the woods forever, when I spot the glint of something shiny, ground level, and suffocated by weeds, and heather, and thigh-high grass. I crouch low, my back already aching as I pick my way through brambles, and stinging nettles, and branches that prick and poke, and claw at the skin on my arms. And then I hear the rumble of a soft growl deep within an animal's chest. My bear-wolf.

I drop to my knees and shuffle into the hollow, the

curtain-branches surrounding us, keeping us safe. I realise I'm still crying, silent tears that sting my raw cheeks, and pummel my forehead from the inside, tears that have no voice because I no longer know what to say.

The creature sniffs Jonah, nudging him with her damp nose. She's unsure. I can sense it in the way her eyes are narrowed, the way her fur feels tight, prickly, and not soft and furry the way I remember.

"It's my baby brother," I whisper. "Jonah. He won't hurt you."

I don't snuggle up to her. I need to be sure Jonah isn't hurt. I sit back, pressed up against her side, my knees raised, and settle him on my legs so I can check nothing is broken. He doesn't cry when I move his arms or his legs and, for a second time, I touch his skull all over with my fingertips. I can't feel anything abnormal, or swollen, or damp with blood, and slowly my breathing calms.

Holding him up to my face I smell him; I can't smell poo. I must ration the few nappies I brought, so I'll only change him when it's desperate, or when he stinks, in case other animals smell him. I have no idea whether that can be dangerous or not, whether it will attract them or not.

In the gloom, I pull my phone out of my pocket and check my messages. I have three missed calls, and my heart flutters. Maybe she's home. But the calls are from Kofi. He's sent five WhatsApp messages.

On the bus. xxx

You okay? Give us a call. xx

Everything ok with our baby? X

Right, now I'm getting worried. Summer?

Summer? Pick up girl come on?

Fresh tears spill out for Kofi. He reminds me of Jonah; he's a pure soul too. Kind. Soft and kind, and it makes me think this is the reason why his stepdad walks all over him. What kind of man stubs out cigarettes on their wife's son? Who does that kind of cruel stuff anyway? The thought of someone doing that to Jonah rips my heart in two. I can't let it happen to him. I can't let him grow up and be treated cruelly, not by anyone, and the slightest whiff of weakness, that's what's going to happen. I've seen it in school. It's why the geeks are picked on. There was a girl in year seven who had to wear glasses with coloured lenses just so she could read, or the words danced all over the page, she said. A popular girl ripped the piss out of her, called her Stevie Wonder or something.

Another message flashes through from Kofi.

You not home? Where you at? X

Still nothing from Mum.

I wonder where she's been and what she'll do when she gets home. Will she accuse Mac the way she did with the strawberry naevus? Maybe she'll think he's kidnapped him? Or maybe she'll just accept he's taken the baby out. Make life easier for her. She might call me, but thinking about it, she'll probably be convinced I've gone to the lantern ceremony, so she'll leave it, expecting me to go out on the piss after with Tia and that lot. Maybe that's where she went wrong. Maybe, just maybe, she should've worried more about what her little girl was doing, instead of thanking her lucky stars she didn't end up with some ugly little cow who preferred books to booze. She doesn't deserve us.

And when she realises that we're not coming back, when Mac comes home reeking of his tart's perfume, and sex-smell, and pretends he hasn't heard from me, she'll cry, and rant, and swear at everyone else, starting with the Ovary, because if I hadn't been made to feel guilty, I wouldn't have run away with her baby. But I don't feel guilty now.

They can blame me for Cee's death all they want, because I know it wasn't my fault, and she's stuck with the man who killed my best friend.

"Ha!" I say out loud. "Ironic."

Another message arrives from Kofi:

On my way to the woods. You with that bear-wolf-thingy of yours? X

"I never blamed you, you know." It's Cee. She must've followed us through the woods. She's stroking Jonah's head, and smiling at me, and I realise this is the first time she's seen my bear-wolf.

"You never believed me," I say.

"Well, you always were a bit crazy," she says. "Like other girls had dolls and kittens, but not you."

"I had dolls. I had a convertible too, and a mansion."

"Course you did." She leans forward and kisses Jonah's cheek. "He smells just like you."

"The best kind of smell." I remember the lantern ceremony. "They're setting off lanterns tonight, in your memory," I say.

She nods. She's still beautiful but in a less vibrant way. A less lively way, like her outline is fading. "It'll be pretty, I guess."

"I can't be there."

"Well, obvs." She laughs. "You're here unless you've discovered time travel."

Jonah wriggles on my lap, but his eyes remain closed, and I wonder if he thinks it's night-time, it's so dark.

"I need to protect him. I don't care if they think I'm a lunatic gone off the rails." I picture the search party, our mum waiting at home by the phone with a supply of nicotine, waiting to hear if they've found us, waiting to sign the forms to have me sectioned. Her wild, uncontrollable daughter. I can't let that happen.

"Ritchie got the pills from Mac," I say.

"I know," she says quickly.

"She doesn't care about Jonah."

"I could've told you that one."

"I'm going to stay here with him. We'll be safe here."

She glances around our hollow, our safe house, our tiny corner of the woods and says, "You can't stay here, Summer. Look at it."

I look around me. Somehow, while we've been speaking, it's changed. My bear-wolf has slunk off into the woods, the soil beneath me is damp and musty, my treasures mouldy and rank, and blood trickles down my arm, where a thorn has caught the flesh and stuck fast. I yank at it and a flap of skin tears loose.

"You can do this, baby girl," she says. "I always knew

you could do it. That's why we were besties." Her smile is so dazzling, for a few seconds it lights up our shadow-cave.

"I'm scared," I say.

"Don't be. Look at him." She nods at Jonah, whose eyes are suddenly open wide, and gazing at me as if I'm his mum. "He trusts you. And I've got your back."

"My bear-wolf is real," I say.

"I know."

"She was supposed to look out for me."

"She did look out for you, but now you have me. Come on, time to go."

My phone pings. Kofi.

Don't you dare leave without me. I'm coming for you xxx

Kofi said he'd had things going on—it's the reason he's been quiet. I didn't ask what things, but that's because I don't need to. Kofi's parents don't deserve him either. A tug of excitement flutters inside my chest; Kofi will never leave me alone. He gets me.

I message him back:

Yell and I'll find you xxx

Cee crawls out of the shadows and into the woods. I tug the bag-straps back onto my shoulder, hug Jonah close to my chest, and follow. The bag is heavier, the straps biting into my shoulder, and my elbow feels numb. It's an effort to crawl outside. To move. I expect her to have vanished too, but she's there, waiting, smiling.

"Where to?" I ask.

She glances left and right. "What are the options?"

I nod in the direction of the river. "That way is south, and home. And this way is north."

"North," she says. "Sounds like an adventure."